and walk now gently through the fire

AND OTHER SCIENCE FICTION STORIES

and walk nou

gently through the fire

AND OTHER SCIENCE FICTION STORIES

edited by ROGER ELWOOD

CHILTON BOOK COMPANY
Philadelphia New York London

Published in Philadelphia by Chilton Book Company
and simultaneously in Ontario, Canada,
by Thomas Nelson & Sons, Ltd.
Manufactured in the United States of America

contents

introduction

By MARSHA DALY

SCIENCE FICTION was once read mainly by impressionable youngsters who, after finishing some particularly dramatic story, would jump around shooting imaginary ray guns and pretending to see through walls (to mention just two such activities). The masters of the genre—H. G. Wells, Jules Verne, Mary Shelley, and others—were tolerated for the superior storytelling powers they manifested but *not* for the astuteness of their scientific extrapolations.

With space achievements and the discovery and refinement of the laser beam and other "wonders," science fiction has assumed its rightful place in the literary world. Suddenly, George Orwell's *1984* (which may be more appropriately dubbed *speculative fantasy*) has ceased to be purely fiction and its totalitarian nightmares have started to evolve into the mainstream of life. Nor are the authors who have dealt with such themes as ecology/pollution, race relations and such been slighted, either, as a casual glance at daily newspapers will confirm.

As science fiction has matured—or could it be that reality has caught up with science fiction?—so has biology. Right now, experiments are being conducted with the *raison d'être* that of finding the secret of life itself, to create life in a test tube. And, hopefully, in the future, geneticists will be able to devise genetic formulas which will eventually eliminate physical and mental deformities.

Yes, man is changing the structure of his world—defying nature in many ways. That is why the college student of today is living in the best of all possible worlds, with society open to ideas, to experimentation. The taboos that once chained men's minds—the theorists of yesterday were met, more often than not, by derisive laughter and forced to endure cruel taunts—have been broken. For now we realize that little is beyond the reach of the human species if our minds are capable of vaulting toward the goal in question.

But what of religion? Has it a place in a scientific world?

Yes! And, again, yes!

More and more scientists are returning to a form of spiritual faith. The men who made the historic first moon flights took time to acknowledge their thanks to a spirit greater than any to be found on earth.

And college students, where once they may have scoffed at admitting to religious beliefs and practices, are coming to place religion on a level with that of science since both search into the unknown for truths.

Science fiction often provides a door to as yet unknown truths in a variety of areas, whether ecology, space travel, population control or whatever; and science fiction *authors* are making young readers think about the future. Somewhere a young man or woman is studying chemistry and reads a story about someone—in science fictiondom—who has discovered a chemical substance that can transform the criminal mind into a force for social stability as opposed to social disruption; and our young chemist's mind becomes fascinated and may ultimately embark on a quest for just such a substance.

And along will come another author who will *question* man's right to interfere with the human condition, an author who will contest the morality of such a move. Consider Anthony Burgess' futuristic novel, *A Clockwork Orange,* and you will find such a classic struggle.

Yet in many areas science and religion can and do live in harmony. Even many scientists have realized that man has need of a soul, be it God-given or man-made (in some way).

There has probably never been a time when students have not

argued for hours in dormitories and cafeterias over religion and its value to our society. Is all life an accident? Is our seeming order the result of some colossal *initial* accident? Has this order and structure through the centuries happened without the guidance of a Supreme Being? On and on the questions—and the discussions. . . .

As in the worlds of biology and religion, strict formats and rigid rules are being phased out of education and it is becoming much more free form. Why? Because the students and progressive teachers feel more freedom will be conducive to creativity.

Breathes there a student anywhere who has not cited the fact that Albert Einstein flunked math at an early age only to create, later, out of his own curiosity and intellectual ability one of the greatest scientific breakthroughs of all time—the theory of relativity?

Here we will study the imaginative outpourings of such science fiction masters as R. A. Lafferty, Robert Silverberg, Barry Malzberg, Robert Bloch, K. M. O'Donnell, Philip José Farmer and Ted White; and such talented genre newcomers as Joan C. Holly, Pamela Sargent and Rachel Payes. This is an anthology that has been compiled by Roger Elwood with an eye toward a variety of tastes. Not everyone is a Lafferty fan, for example, but his contribution herein could be his best short work to date—and one to be reckoned with at Nebula Awards time; not everyone will go for the rather fundamental Christianity in Joan Holly's novelette but it is a sincere and impeccably written story just the same; and some readers will not appreciate the diary format of K. M. O'Donnell's contribution but we feel this is a hallmark work. The styles and approaches herein are diverse; and is that not one of the advantages of the anthology format: to present a cross section of literary roads by which the authors feel compelled to travel.

No doubt one of you—or many more, perhaps—reading this book will find your mind opened to new horizons. And perhaps herein you will be motivated to study, further, biology and/or religion because a certain hypothesis strikes your fancy.

Or you may seek and find only pure entertainment. Whichever is the case, we hope you agree that this anthology is one of the finest in recent years.

and walk now gently through the fire

AND OTHER SCIENCE FICTION STORIES

stella

By TED WHITE

Transcript of statement made by Howard Higgins to Dr. William Knight, staff psychotherapist, Federal Land Bureau, Dept. M.

ALL RIGHT. It was against the rules. I knew that. We both knew it. But you have to look at it from our point of view. Clara had wanted a baby so badly. A long time before we shipped out, Doc Bradley told us the odds against a successful pregnancy were better than fifty to one. That's what I had to live with—can you blame me for taking a chance?

It seemed like a miracle when we found her out back in the brush that day. It was Clara who found her, actually. I was working on a loose valve on the steamplow, my hands blistering with the heat, and I heard her calling out from back in the brush.

"Howard—*Howard!* Come quick! Oh, come *see!*" It's damned quiet out here beyond Fredricsburg—sometimes the stillness really gets to me, that's when I get homesick for Earth—and Clara's voice rang like a bell. Sounded too excited to be just an accident of some kind, and besides which she'd learned her lesson with the honeybush that time—skin grafts are painful and more effective than my yelling at her all the time to be careful. She didn't sound hurt anyway, nor frightened. Just excited—*happy*, maybe.

So I laid down my tools, very neatly on the groundcloth, the way I always do, and I straightened up to get the cricks out of my back, and then I made my way across the spring furrows for the far side of the field and the wild brush beyond.

I'm a careful man; you want to take that into account. It's Clara who goes poking around bumping into honeybushes and getting into trouble. I'm a farmer, just a transplanted New England boy trying to make a go of a new farm here on this unholy planet, fighting a sun that's too small and too blue and wants to burn half my crops and a soil that looks rich enough but has the molecules in its trace elements all hooked up wrong—"lefthanded," the man from the Land Bureau puts it—so that everything has to be done all over again from scratch.

So I walk—I never run. And I take my time, so's I don't get out of breath. And all this time Clara is crying out, calling for me to hurry up, get a move on, and come see what it is she's just found. I figured if it hadn't already gone away with all the noise she was making, it would wait for me to get there, and I was right.

It was a baby.

Just lying there, all wrapped in a silky wrapping—"like swaddling clothes" was the way it came to me then—under this big bush we called a "cabbage bush" because that's what it looks like. The baby wasn't crying or anything, and for a moment I thought it wasn't real—like it was somebody's idea of a mean joke on us, putting a plastic baby out here where we'd find it, on account of how Clara and I wanted a baby so bad, which was well known. Even putting it under a cabbage bush—didn't they used to say, a long time ago on Earth, that you found babies under the cabbage plants? I remember my grandmother saying that once. So I was feeling my temper starting to rise, thinking about the kind of person who would do something like that to us, and me with a broken steamplow to take care of anyway; and then she opened her eyes and looked at me.

"Look at it, Howard! Isn't it sweet? I wanted you to see it just the way I found it—I haven't even touched it!"

"Where'd that baby come from?" I asked, and I guess my voice was a little gruff.

"Why, Howard! How should *I* know? Somebody must have left it here."

"Sure," I said. "People all the time leave babies out here behind our farm."

"Howard," she said, and she had an edge in her voice which I took special note of, because Clara is not given to raising her voice except on special occasions. "I have no idea how this baby came to be here, and I don't know who could have left it here. But here it is, Howard. A baby. For *us.*" She stooped and picked the baby up, holding it in her arms very protectively, as though I might try and take it from her. "This is *our* baby now, Howard," she said.

Well, that's how we found her. I prowled around the area, but there was no sign of anything to explain how she got there. Just this little nest of old cabbage bush leaves, with her lying in the middle wrapped in silk wrappings. She never made a sound—never did, either—but just looked at us with sky-blue eyes, wide and wondering, like any newborn baby child in the world.

We took her back up to the house and Clara unwrapped her—which is how we found out she was a girl-baby—and we looked at her tiny body and tried to figure what we were going to do with her.

Clara never had any doubts in her mind. "We're keeping her, and that's that!"

"We'll have to tell them at the Land Bureau," I said. "And how are we to take care of a tiny baby like this, anyway?"

"You won't tell a single soul, Howard Higgins—not till we're good and ready! Now, right now I want you to find us something we can use as a crib. I can't just sit here holding the little darling all day."

"But—she'll have to be fed!"

"You let me worry about that. You go find her a crib."

Just to look at the two of us, you'd never doubt I was the man in charge of our family. But when it comes right down to it, that's because Clara is happy to let me take care of most things and there's no arguments. We both work hard and we both trust each other. That's the way a marriage should be, to my way of thinking. But now here we were with this baby all of a sudden, and everything was topsy-turvy.

I looked over what was at hand and decided nothing would do, as is. So I spent the next hour putting together a wooden box with legs, the legs on wide rockers (so it wouldn't rock too far and tip over), and then spraying on a fresh coat of lacquer. Nothing like what my father, who was a cabinetmaker wintertimes back in New Hampshire, could do but it sufficed.

Clara used an extra pillow for a mattress in the crib, and the silken wrappings made a nice cover. She cut up some lengths of cheesecloth, folded over a few times, for diapers. And there we were, all set to keep and raise that little girl just like she was already our own. I didn't like it; it just didn't seem right.

Just to show you how much this whole business fuddled me that first day, I didn't even remember that damned steamplow until it was bright afternoon, and the sun too high to even think about going back out to the field. I wasted most of a day, that day—didn't get the thing fixed and running until dusk, and didn't finish plowing in the Earth phosphates until the next day.

"Her name is Stella," Clara told me that night. We were sitting outside on the open porch, digesting our supper, and I was rocking the crib with my foot. The measured cadence lulled me, but the minimal effort—moving my foot—left me only half-drowsing.

"What?" I said, feeling jerked awake by the sound of her voice, wondering if I'd missed an essential exchange in the previous moment.

"I've been thinking about a name for her. We can't just go on calling her 'the baby,' you know."

"Stella sounds like the kind of a woman we, umm, wouldn't associate with, back home. I don't like it. Besides, who are we to be naming the baby? I told you, tomorrow I'm going to have to go into Fredricsburg. . . ."

"Nonsense. Tomorrow you have to finish the plowing."

"The next day, then. But they'll have to be told. The baby could be missing—kidnapped, or something."

"I don't believe it."

"Clara," I said, "listen to me. Babies don't appear under cabbage bushes, just like that. Some woman bore that baby, and recently, too. You think about that: somewhere there's a mother who doesn't have her baby any more."

I thought that would get to her, but I reckoned without her stubbornness. "Howard, I am well aware that she did not grow overnight under that silly bush. Somebody put her there. Now you think about *this:* Somebody had that little baby and they didn't want her. No, it could easily happen! You know the sorts of people there are in Fredricsburg these days, ever since the Army set up that big base . . . well, never mind about that. What counts is that they brought her here—to us. They didn't want a baby, and we do."

"You're saying somebody knew that?"

"Why not? It's no secret."

"So they figured we'd care for her if they didn't, hmmm?"

"What better reason?"

"Why didn't they just leave her on our doorstep? Why'd they leave her out back, in the brush, where we mightn't have found her for days? Eh?"

"I'm sure I don't know, but maybe it happened they were afraid."

"Afraid?" I snorted. "Of what?"

"Afraid they'd be seen—afraid we'd give her back."

"I don't believe it," I said, and I didn't.

"That's as may be. It doesn't matter. We're keeping her."

"And you want to call her Stella?"

She smiled. "Can't we, Howard?"

So I didn't go into town the next day—I finished the plowing instead. And the next day there was other work to be done, and so on, so that a week passed by and we'd told no one about the baby we'd found out back.

And in that time we began to adjust to the changes in our routine, and the little child became part of them, part of *us* really, so that it grew easier to put off doing something about her, about telling the authorities about her. Mind you, I was never entirely easy in my mind about what we were doing, but I could see what having her meant to Clara and that made a lot of difference.

She wasn't a difficult baby, either. Not like some people's children, waking up in the middle of the night, crying, throwing up, things like that. Maybe that should've made me uneasy too, but it didn't. Not then.

She never cried. She never made a sound. She would lie for hours in her rocking crib, her eyes wide and staring, hardly ever stirring. It wasn't something I took much notice of, not right away. I was too busy and I saw her only for short times during the day. Clara had mixed up a formula for her, of milk with a little honey in it, and she used an old rubber glove (which she boiled before using), with a small hole in one finger, to feed the baby. It looked a little odd, that red rubber glove full of milk like a balloon, with one finger stuck in the baby's mouth, but it certainly seemed to work. Clara said the baby gained two pounds in just that first week.

You'll notice I don't call the baby Stella. I never could. It's not a pretty name to me, not a nice name; there are probably lots of perfectly nice women named Stella, but I never knew any, and that's what mattered to me then. Later I just couldn't think of her as ever growing up to be a woman named Stella, because I knew better.

It took me a month to figure out that something was wrong with the baby. That's because I haven't had much experience with babies, and you want to remember that I had a full work schedule anyway. It was early spring and I had crops to get in. Everything has to be up and harvested by early summer, because nothing grows in the searingly hot full summer months here. Nothing I *want* to grow, anyway. Spring and fall are the growing seasons—and we're lucky this planet has a long year.

I'd gotten used to holding the baby, though. Clara insisted on that. She'd give me the baby to hold after supper, and we'd sit out on the porch and I'd rock in my favorite chair with the baby sort of cuddled up in my arms. It was a nice feeling, you know—holding a helpless little bundle like that.

But one evening I said something to Clara about her. It was just a chance remark, really, because I hadn't been thinking that much about it. "She's sure a quiet baby," I said. "I kinda expected she'd move about more, now."

"What do you mean?" Clara asked, that little edge in her voice that told me I was venturing into dangerous waters.

"Oh, nothing much," I said, in what I hoped was a reassuring voice. Clara had been possessive about the baby since the day we'd found her, but if anything she was even more possessive about her now. "It's just that I thought babies, umm, squirmed more." I chucked her under her tiny chin with my forefinger, and she stared up at me with dreamy eyes. "Or maybe grabbed at things, you know what I mean? When do babies start grabbing things?"

"Howard, Stella is just an *infant*. She's just a tiny newborn baby. You can't expect her to be doing all those things yet." Her voice seemed a little uncertain.

"Now, Clara, we've had her for a month now. You can't be calling her 'newborn' any more. And we don't know how old she was when we found her. She wasn't all red or anything, like they say they are when they're born."

"Of course not! That doesn't last more than a few hours. But she's still *very* young, and you can't expect much of her at this age."

"Well, all right. But are you sure you're feeding her properly? Is she—?"

I shouldn't have said that. Clara got angrier than I've ever seen her, grabbed the baby from me, and shooed me off the porch. She was still shouting about how much weight the baby had gained, and what a fool I was when I slammed the door on her in pure disgust. It was the closest to a fight we'd had in all the years we'd been married.

I put it down to nerves on Clara's part, but I couldn't stop thinking about it. It didn't seem natural the way that baby just lay there all the time, never struggling, never really moving much, just lying there and staring at things in that unfocussed, baby way. Babies fuss and they squirm and they grab at things. Man told me once that babies have an instinct about grabbing on—something left over from when we were all apes and they could grab on to their mother's fur. "One of the first things a baby learns to do," I recall him saying, "is to make a fist. When a baby gets mad, it makes a fist."

Our baby—I thought of her by then as "our baby," even if I knew better in the back of my mind—never closed her perfect tiny fingers into a fist. But then, she never seemed to get mad about anything either.

I'll tell you my first thought about her then, and it was that she was defective—brain damaged, maybe. It would go a long way towards explaining why she'd been left out there in the brush. They have ways of finding these things out now, and if she'd been born defective, they'd have known and maybe her parents just decided not to keep her. I'd heard of things like that. Raising a defective child can be more than some folks can abide. It made sense, their putting her out there in the brush. She might be found, she might not. They were leaving it up to chance. It made sense to me, thinking it through like that.

Otherwise, she seemed perfectly healthy. Clara said she had a good appetite, and Clara weighed her regularly, every day. She even kept a chart of the baby's weight, and later on that night she showed it to me to prove to me she'd been feeding her properly. That night, after we'd gone to bed, she talked to me about it, and told me she was sorry she'd gone off like that; it wasn't like her and she hadn't known what was in her. But I figured she was worried too, and doing her best not to admit to it.

I took the hopper into Fredricsburg late that spring. The baby was about four months old by then, and something was obviously wrong with her. Clara's fingers went white as she gripped my arm before I left, and she asked me to see if I could have a word with Doc Bradley without saying more'n I had to.

I was going in to arrange for the collection and shipment of our cash crop, soybeans, but I had it in the back of my mind to see what I could find out about our baby's condition while I was there.

She still lay about, docile and uncomplaining, but she was no longer an infant. She'd completely outgrown her rocker-crib a month earlier, and I'd built her a bed, like a real bed but quarter-sized. It didn't need sides, because she never rolled over.

She was big—much too big, I thought. She weighed thirty-five pounds, and Clara had to strain when she bent over to lift her out of her bed or lower her back in. She still sucked honeyed milk from the glove, but with a voracious appetite. She drank more than a gallon a day—and we were nearly out of the bulk powder, one more reason for my trip into town.

She was big, but she hadn't *developed* at all. I couldn't figure it. It was as if she had *expanded*—the proportions were exactly the same as they'd been the first day we'd found her. Her legs were still short, her head seemed much too large, and her arms flopped uselessly at her side. We'd tried exercising her, but it was like exercising a rag doll. She didn't protest—she never protested—but she remained completely limp.

Clara was convinced now that the baby had suffered some sort of brain damage—that she was paralyzed, in fact. I started out thinking that too, but it didn't fit—not quite. Because I've seen four-month-old babies. It isn't just that by then they're starting to crawl; their legs are longer, and their other body proportions have also changed. Our baby's hadn't.

I made a point of stopping at Doc Bradley's after I'd taken care of my business in Fredricsburg, and I told him I wanted to see a text book on babies—preferably one with pictures.

"Kinda late in life for you to work up an interest in babies, Howard," he said. "Let me see what I've got. Hmmm . . . Haycock & Morris' *Baby Atlas* . . . this the sort thing you're looking for?"

It was. I flipped through the early pages; our baby looked pretty much like most newborns. But midway through the second chapter—two and three months—I stopped and began looking at each picture.

It was as I'd suspected: confirmation. Our baby hadn't really changed at all—she'd just grown larger. Suddenly I was struck by the memory of an old joke—a sick joke a man had once told me about a baby which grew as big as a house without ever ceasing to be a baby.

"What is it, Howard? You look as if you'd seen a ghost." Bradley peered over my shoulder at the page I was staring at, but I wasn't looking at the pictures of the babies. I was seeing *her*, the baby Clara called Stella, a monstrously bloated caricature of a newborn infant, but four months old.

I shook my head and slammed the book shut. "I don't know, Doc," I said. "I just don't know."

"You'd better tell me, then," he said, easing a chair behind my knees. I sank back into it and tried to order my thoughts. I am in most circumstances a careful, orderly man, and not easily confused. But I found it difficult to speak at that moment, less because I had nothing to say than because I was unsure of *how* to say it. Finally I just blurted it out—and the devil with the consequences.

"Doc, we've got this baby."

His eyes widened, then he grinned. "Congratulations, but aren't I seeing the wrong person? Where's your wife?"

"Out on the farm—with the baby."

"Out on the—? Now wait a minute, Howard. Are you trying to tell me she's *had* the baby? I saw Clara just last—when was it?" He started counting on his fingers. "That was when she came in for her pap test, and. . . ."

"Uhh, Doc, hold it. Uh-uh. I didn't say Clara had a baby. Not *that* way. We found it. Out back."

"You *found* a baby?"

I told him the whole story, beginning to end, including my original theories about the baby's abandonment. I felt a lot better, telling someone about the whole thing. Confession was good for my soul, I guess—and telling him wasn't the same as going to the Land Bureau with it. So I just poured it out and he sat there and listened, interrupting only once in a while when he wasn't sure about something, the expression on his face gradually changing from the original smile to a puzzled frown. When I'd finished, he frowned some more.

"I think the first order of the day is to track down the baby's real parents," he said at last. "Find out their history, see what we can find out about this condition. And, of course, you'll have to bring her in for me to look her over."

I shook my head. "Nope. That's out. Clara wouldn't stand for it."

"But, good god, man! You can't just go on like this forever! That's not a normal baby you've been hiding out there. It needs help. It needs medical attention!"

I sighed. "Sure, I know that. But . . . Clara. . . ."

He nodded, his shoulders suddenly slumping. "Yes. Clara. She's pretty obsessed with it, isn't she?"

"You know how long she's wanted a baby, Doc. And at her age. . . ."

"Will she let me see it—if I come out, I mean?"

"Could you?"

"I can't see any other way around it. I'll have to do some checking here first, of course. Birth records, that sort of thing. Unless someone delivered the baby themselves. . . ." He looked tired. "I'll see what I can find out, then I'll drop in on you. How's that?"

"If you could make it like a, well, a social visit . . . ?"

He held out his hand. "We'll play it by ear," he said.

That's where we left it. I was to expect him some time in the next week—it wasn't easy to pry him loose from the demands of his practice on short notice, he reminded me—and he would say nothing about what I'd already told him. I had to trust him on that, but Doc Bradley was an easy man to trust.

I stayed over that night in Fredricsburg at the Public House. Hank Levey and Gardner Pritchet were there that night, having come in to town on errands similar to mine. They're fellow farmers, although not neighbors, and we spent a few hours trading complaints about the Land Bureau. Gardner is a dour man, originally from upstate New York, and as little convinced now as he was twenty years ago that man was ever meant to try farming on an alien planet where even the most familiar looking things can turn out to have unsuspected repercussions. "We've just scratched at the surface of this place," he said at one point. "Why, nine-tenths of this planet haven't even been explored."

"Now, Gardner," Hank said. Hank is inclined to heaviness which working under a blue sun hasn't yet sweated off him, but he's the most gentle man I've ever met. "You know quite well the Land Bureau has mapped the whole face of this planet."

"Sure it has—from satellites miles out in space. What does that tell you? Where the rivers are? Why, how long ago did we happen on them voles? Just four years ago—and they like to wiped out every crop I had. Where was the Land Bureau *then,* I'm asking you?"

The voles are little animals, not much bigger than mice, apparently mammals. Nobody ever saw one before that year—and suddenly they were all over everywhere. They're under control now, but nobody has said yet where they'd been all those years before, or what triggered them off like that.

"That's just something you want to expect on a new planet," Hank pointed out, very reasonably. "You want to *expect* a surprise now and then."

But we didn't—not really. Not then.

Clara was distraught when I got home the next day.

"Oh, Howard! I'm so glad you're back! I hardly slept at all last night —it's Stella!"

I did my best to calm her down and try to make sense of what she was saying, but it wasn't until I looked at the baby that I began to share her feelings.

She was lying in her bed as usual, and for the first moment she looked to me like just an ordinary baby, just a little tiny girl asleep in her crib. Then Clara raised the shades and as the harsh light struck her, I saw what had so upset my wife.

Her skin was darkening. It was a light greenish-brown.

"What's this?" I demanded. "How did this happen?"

"I don't *know,*" she wailed. "It started last night—that's when I first noticed it. I thought it was the light, but it wasn't. She—her skin—it was green looking. I thought she might be sick, but she didn't have a temperature. But she's—she's *sleeping*. She's been sleeping ever since! She hasn't eaten a drop!"

"Has she opened her eyes at all?"

"No, and she won't, either."

"What do you mean?"

"I—I tried to open one eye—you know the way—? And I *couldn't.*"

I leaned over the little bed. In repose her infant's face was innocent of all expression—not that it ever betrayed much emotion. I let my thumb rest lightly on her eye, my hand cupped against her cheek. I tried to thumb her eyelid up. It wouldn't move. I leaned closer. My thumb brushed against her tiny eyelashes. They fell out.

Clara screamed.

I had my hands full with Clara for the next hour and a half, just trying to get her calmed down. I'm not much for handling a woman in hysterics. I finally dumped a bucket of water over her, and that did the trick. "What did you do that for?" she asked, but in a much subdued voice.

Well, with one thing and another, I didn't get back to looking at the baby for quite a while. When I did, it seemed to me that her skin had turned darker. It looked browner, less green tinged. I shook my head; it made no sense to me.

I remembered her lashes falling out—that being what had triggered Clara—and took another look. Try as I might, I couldn't find a seam where her upper lid met the lower. It was all just smooth skin. I ran my fingers through her short hair, and it didn't surprise me as much when it fell out, too.

Her skin felt warm to the touch, but not feverish. It also felt smoother, somehow less yielding. On a hunch, I checked her breathing. It had stopped. So had her pulse. And her lips, like her eyes, were welded together. I shone a light into her nose; her nostrils were plugged with something brownish just inside.

When I tell you these things now, it's impossible to describe how I felt when I was first observing them. I've gone through too much since—it just doesn't mean anything to me anymore, not like it did then. Mostly I didn't want to say anything to Clara, because I was afraid of what she might do. I just examined the baby like I would a soil sample and kept my thoughts to myself.

We didn't get much done that day. The hours had gone rapidly; and after Clara's hysterics, evening-time was real close. We skipped supper. I found some leftovers and ate them cold without paying much attention to them and I couldn't even tell you now what they were—and we just sat around looking at nothing much and not saying anything. Every so often I'd go look at the baby, just to see if anything else had happened, but nothing had, unless she'd grown another couple of shades darker. Finally, somewhere around dusk, I went out to the tool shed and began taking out and cleaning everything and putting it all back again, and that took up my time until we went to bed. I don't know what Clara did during that time.

In the morning I woke up with the feeling that the whole thing had just been a bad dream. But when I went into the baby's room, it was to face the fact that this was no dream at all.

She was black.

Ebony black, I think the phrase goes. I've never seen ebony, but her skin was jet black, completely black, with just maybe the hint of green if the light was just right. But that might have been my eyes. Her skin was black and satin-shiny, not polished looking, but like old wood with a good finish to it. She looked like a perfectly carved statue of a baby, larger than life-sized.

I stared at her and then I reached out and touched her, very lightly.

Her skin was hard. Still warm, body warm, but stone hard, unyielding.

"It's too late to help her, isn't it?" Clara asked from the doorway behind me. "We should have gotten the doctor, shouldn't we?"

I shook my head. "It wouldn't have helped." If I'd turned right around and gone back to Fredricsburg I couldn't have gotten Doc Bradley back in time. "Besides, this isn't anything a doctor could do something about. You know that."

"What do you mean?"

"It's crazy," I said. Wrong word—but fortunately, she didn't react. "This isn't a normal baby. It never was. The way we found it wasn't normal. How could a doctor treat a baby for something like this?"

"They've got computers. . . ."

I snorted in disgust. "A fancy medical library in solid state storage. You think the computers ever heard of something like this?"

"Earth might–"

"Earth is a month away. Forget Earth. They can't help us."

"Who can? Oh, Howard, I'm so frightened for her. She was just a little baby!"

I put my arms around her bony shoulders and held her and she cried into my chest. I'd never seen her cry before, not like this.

All we could do was watch. In my mind I thought of it as a death watch, but I kept that to myself. The baby's body remained warm; life in some mysterious way still persisted. She neither breathed nor moved; she was stiff and apparently lifeless, a statue. But yet some spark remained that told me she was not dead. We could only wait and watch and wonder.

That afternoon, when the heat had abated a little, I went out to tend to the neglected chores and for a few hours I lost myself in simple back breaking, bone wearying work. It was a pleasure and a relief. I returned to the house almost reluctantly, knowing no hope, expecting no change.

Clara wasn't in the kitchen where I'd expected to find her. I went straight to the baby's room. She wasn't there. I almost didn't look into the baby's bed, but something warned me and I turned back.

A shiver of cold touched my spine. The bed was empty. I hurried out of the room.

I found them both in the little room Clara used as a sewing room, too small for anything but a fabricator and a large old chest of drawers which had been in her family for generations and which she'd refused to leave behind us when we'd shipped from Earth. She was standing in the center of the room, holding the baby tight against her chest, slowly rocking back and forth with it, and crooning softly.

I stopped just outside the open door, unwilling to intrude. As I stood there, motionless, I realized that Clara was saying the baby's name over and over, "Stel-la, Stel-la, Stel-la. . . ." making it into a tuneless sort of song.

Finally I had to move and as I did I made some noise, startling her.

She whirled, and as she did the baby slipped from her arms. She shrieked–as if in premonition–and the baby fell to the floor.

And shattered.

Like a porcelain figurine, the baby's body broke into pieces, bursting and releasing its liquid contents, spattering over Clara, onto my legs, filling the small room with the bilious stuff.

Clara collapsed in a swoon from which I caught her just before she hit the floor.

They came out to see us two days later, but much too late.

Doc Bradley was with them, but he said little. They came in an official hopper, three men from the Land Bureau and the Under Commissioner himself. I wasn't expecting any of them so soon, but you couldn't say I was surprised. I was past surprise.

I had occupied myself well. I had done all the things which had needed to be done. I had cleaned Clara and put her to bed, keeping her there under sedation, feeding her myself with broth. I had done each day's necessary farm work, mostly readying the harvest for transportation. And I had saved samples—in the deep-freeze—of the blackened shell and thick liquid which bespattered Clara's sewing room, each neatly labeled and ready for analysis. Nothing was wanting in that regard, and I'm sure they were grateful for it. I had, of course, completely cleaned the room afterwards.

I showed them the samples and they nodded wisely and while they were conferring among themselves Doc Bradley took me aside and explained their presence. "You see how it is, Howard. I checked the birth records quite thoroughly, and there simply *weren't* any babies unaccounted for. I even talked to Dr. Vorzimer—he takes care of the, ah, girls, out at the Army base—and there just wasn't any way we could account for the baby you found. Well, at that point I had to go to the Bureau—you can see that. I was still hoping for a nice simple, easy answer. However. . . ." and he sighed, gustily. "I'd better see to your wife, now."

Clara is back on Earth now, and they tell me I'll be able to see her regularly when I get back. I've sold the farm back to the Land Bureau and it's just a matter of time before they'll be finished with me here. They tell me that these sessions with you are just a formality, what with Clara and all, to assure my own fitness. I don't know what I can tell you beyond what I've already said. Doc Bradley told me last night that

I'm in a state of mild shock but that it'll wear off eventually. I'm luckier, or maybe tougher, than Clara, I guess.

Transcript of an interview between Howard Higgins and Dr. Gregory Benford, staff biochemist, Federal Land Bureau, Dept. D:

BENFORD: Have they explained to you the purpose of this interview?

HIGGINS: Uhm, yessir, they said you could tell me what happened. To the, uh, the baby, I mean.

BENFORD: That's right. But first I want to ask you if you're familiar with the life processes of common insects.

HIGGINS: On Earth, you mean?

BENFORD: Yes. And here.

HIGGINS: I don't know. . . .

BENFORD: All right. We'll start there.

HIGGINS: But what—?

BENFORD: Just let me explain; it'll make sense if you hear me out. All right?

HIGGINS: Okay.

BENFORD: Right. There are two basic types of insects—those which go through a larval stage, to a pupal stage and an adult stage—and those which don't. Cockroaches don't, for instance. But most insects do. Are you familiar with the mechanism involved?

HIGGINS: Uhm, no sir, I don't think I ever knew, one way or the other. I mean, I know about the larval stage—that's like caterpillars, right? And them turning into butterflies. But. . . .

BENFORD: All right. Basically such an insect is two separate life forms living in a symbiotic arrangement. The larval form and the adult form are not only separate and distinct from each other, they have separate genetic codes and can evolve independently of each other, to meet seperate environmental demands. Do you follow? The larval stage—say a caterpillar—can, through evolutionary pressures, change colors, change its diet, or do whatever necessary to adapt and survive as a caterpillar. Whatever changes it makes to meet conditions—these changes have nothing to do with the adult stage, which must deal with different conditions, and usually a different environment. Similarly, the adult stage can also evolve independently of the larval stage.

This is because the genetic makeup of each is separate and distinct. The fact is, each, ah, "newborn" insect is not one, but *two* living creatures. The larval stage is the first to develop, but inside the larval stage are separate groups of cells—the embryonic *adult* insect. These cells do not develop, but remain dormant throughout the growth of the larval stage of the insect. Do you follow me, thus far?

HIGGINS: Yes, but what has this to do with—?

BENFORD: Bear with me. There are other differences between the two cell groups. The embryonic larval cells grow, but they do not *multiply*. That is, the larval stage is completely formed, in embryo, so to speak. Each cell grows larger as the insect feeds, but the number of cells does not change. This is why the larval stages of most insects are simpler, their cells less specialized in function. Most larval insects exist solely to eat, to grow as large as possible. That is their sole function.

The adult stage cells, on the other hand, can multiply. When the larval stage ceases and the insect goes into its pupal stage, a hormone is triggered which releases a digestive enzyme. All the larval cells are dissolved into a sort of "soup." At this point the adult cells begin to multiply, feeding off this "soup." When the process is complete, the adult emerges, whole and ready to mate and begin the whole cycle again. Many adult insects do not eat at all, but mate and die, exhausted.

HIGGINS: All this stuff you've just told me—are you trying to say our baby was—?

BENFORD: —a larval stage. Yes.

HIGGINS: But she was *human!* I mean, all right, maybe she wasn't human. Maybe she's alien—something native to this planet, I don't know. . . . But she was a *mammal*. She had soft skin, and you could feel her bones, and she drank milk! You can't tell me she was an *insect*. I won't—

BENFORD: Mr. Higgins, that is exactly what I am trying to tell you. We've done some fairly exhaustive tests on those samples you saved, and there is no doubt in our minds. The, ah, "baby" you found was the larval stage of a native insectoid creature.

HIGGINS: But, *how?*

BENFORD: That's a difficult question to answer right now, but I would say we're uncovering evidence of an amazing evolutionary leap. The picture that we have right now looks like this.

At some point in the distant past of this planet, an insectoid life form developed the capacity to mimic the young of a mammalian life form. This is probably because the larval stage of the insectoid was in danger from emerging mammals—it may have been a good food source. That's just my guess. The answer was, "If you can't beat 'em, join 'em." The larval stage learned to mimic the mammalian newborns, and thus was fed and raised by the mammalian parents.

Now the process by which this mimicry was carried out is fascinating! Apparently the larval insectoid learned to crack the mammalian genetic code! Through a cell sample, a tissue scraping of some sort, probably performed by the adult insectoid in conjunction with mating, the larval insectoid was able to develop a cell structure identical to that of an embryonic mammal. However, the cells of the *adult* insectoid remained unchanged.

HIGGINS: Then our baby was–?

BENFORD: –the product of an adult insectoid which had obtained, somehow, human cell tissue with which to work.

HIGGINS: But how? I've never seen anything like what you're talking about. You're saying that our baby was a larva–what kind of insect would've hatched out of a thirty-five-pound larva?

BENFORD: I wish I knew. We have no records of any human-insectoid contacts–no records of any insect life form of this planet that large, in fact. But of course we really know very little about the life forms indigenous to this planet, despite the time we've been here. Can you think of any opportunity you or your wife might have given *any* native life form to gain tissue samples?

HIGGINS: In what way?

BENFORD: Oh, falling, scraping skin off your knee–bleeding, even. I don't know. (Sighs) You'll be leaving soon, Mr. Higgins, but our staff has only begun its work here. It's like looking for a needle in a haystack. I realize. . . .

HIGGINS: No, wait a minute. I just thought–what about that honeybush?

BENFORD: Honeybush?

HIGGINS: Clara lost a lot of skin on a honeybush out back. . . .

BENFORD: That's a possibility.

HIGGINS: But that would mean . . .

BENFORD: What?

HIGGINS: If they were working with Clara's cells . . . if the, um, the larva was based on Clara's cells . . .

BENFORD: Yes?

HIGGINS: Then she–it–it was really her baby!

BENFORD: Assuming that your wife was the cell donor, yes. It's a cloning sort of thing. . . .

HIGGINS: Sweet Jesus Christ. (prayerfully)

BENFORD: We'd certainly like to find more of these "babies." We'd like to grow one to adulthood, just to see. . . . Mr. Higgins? Mr. Higgins! Where are you going? I have some more questions. . . .

End of interview. Recommended for transmission to Earth Federal, priority frequencies.

making it through

By BARRY N. MALZBERG

1.

"BACK TO GANYMEDE," I think the Captain says somewhat drunkenly, his eyes rotating unevenly within their mad orbit, "back to the base. We must tell them what has happened to us. Lord save us from the sons of bitches. My—my mind is reeling. Sa, sa, sa," and takes a concealed knife from a bulkhead, lurches toward me. I slap the knife from his quivering hand with careless ease, drop him to the panels with a blow and do what I can to lash him with ropes. Unquestionably he has gone mad. This does not fill me with panic so much as a querulous nostalgia: now as never before I remember the Captain as he was in his sane periods and he was everything a Captain should be: stolid, efficient, sexually repressed. Now it is all different.

The arthopods of Jupiter have gotten to him, exactly as rumored. Malevolent, mysterious, they have brought their strange powers to bear upon him and the Captain has crumpled. My own resistance level seems to be somewhat higher but then, on the other hand, one never knows.

2.

The arthopods of Jupiter, the best scientific informants have advised us, possess a secret and pervasive weapon of enormous range and total penetration: it breaks down the amino acids upon contact to produce all of the classic symptoms of the archaic disease, schizophrenia. Three exploratory flights have gone and returned with their crew totally insane: now it is our chance. We have been given further shielding, deliberate instructions, history of the symptomology, drug therapy, tests for resistance. It is hoped that these preparations will make our mission successful and we will be able to conquer the dread arthopods of Jupiter and claim that planet, as so many others, for mankind. All that we have to do is to settle in orbit and use the incendiary devices prepared for us. All life on Jupiter will perish under atomic bombardment and the way to the planet will lie clearly before us. All that we have to do is to settle in orbit and use the devices. Utilize one simple control and that will be the end of the arthopods, the only suspected sentient life on Jupiter. We need, we have been advised, the living space. Yet, despite all these preparations, the Captain's sanity has already collapsed and my own is preserved only by this careful set of notes which I will keep straight through. I will keep them straight through. One simple control is all I have to push.

3.

"Double up for comfort," the mad Captain sings, now lashed to the floor, "they could have sent us one by one at less risk and expense but they have a crew so that no one can trust anyone else. To report on each other. A crew of two for me and you," the Captain murmurs and makes a series of fishlike struggles against the bindings, gives that up, and motions me to him with a demented wink. "Listen here," he says. "You know they're all out to get us: the administrators, the colony, everyone. How can we tell the aliens from the enemies? Turn around and go back there. Use the explosives on them. That's a direct order, you son of a bitch," he says and caresses my cheekbone with a careful finger. I feel a suspicion of sexual response; I have become very attached to the Captain. "No," I say, *"no,"* and leave his side, remembering the dread persuasiveness of the paranoid schizophrenic; his ability to conjure a reality which matches his own construct. We will be within orbit in a matter of hours; I must retain control just long enough to use the devices and destroy the arthopods. Then I, too, may have the pleasure of going mad if I wish.

4.

The ray of the arthopods, we have been told, is their only defensive mechanism. They are a shy, stupid race, somewhat less intelligent than horses who graze amid the gases of Jupiter and routinely emit this ray as a skunk might emit odor, with no more sensibility. We need not be concerned about their elimination. Jupiter is a fertile world and we need the space. Schizophrenia is reversible although the kind of schizophrenia which the arthopods induce has not responded to any treatment so far.

5.

The Captain evinces the blunted affect and ideas of reference common to chronic undifferentiated schizophrenia. "Look here," he says to me with stunning persuasiveness, marred only slightly by the indignity of his position. "I'm not insane. *You* are. I'm the Captain and far more biologically resistant to the ray. You've gone insane and are showing a paranoid reaction. This is not a mission of destruction. Please listen to me. We are on a mission of investigation; to study the arthopods who are a highly intelligent race if a slightly clumsy one and to make overtures of accommodation to them. These atomic devices we carry are only for self-defense. You have become schizophrenic, paranoid type and believe that we must destroy the arthopods and with the muscularity of the demented have overpowered me before I could protect myself. Please listen to me. Please release me and go to your room. I will turn the flight around and we will return. I will take no retaliatory action against you. You are a sick man. You have a terrible disease."

"No," I say with the impassivity necessary to confront the schizoid, "you are wrong. You have gone mad and I retain a wedge on sanity. We are to wipe out the arthopods and you are cunningly trying to turn it the other way. I will not listen to you anymore. Twenty minutes now before we slide into orbit and then I will press the button. I will wipe the buggers out of the solar system because they are evil."

"No, you have it wrong," the Captain says, now whimpering a bit, his control evading him. "You are quite mad. I am sane. Please release me."

"No," I say. "This mission will succeed. I will not be deterred. I am more resistant."

And so on and so forth; our discussion, querulous and bitter by turns, continuing as we approach the point of orbit. It will not be much longer now. Not much longer. "Surely we deserve the solar system," I say. "That's the least I can ask for our trouble getting this far."

6.

To steel myself and retain my perspective, I inscribe the six forms of the old disease schizophrenia: hebephrenic, simple type, catatonic, paranoid, chronic undifferentiated, and schizo-affective. Catatonia is the deadliest, chronic undifferentiated the most insidious. Schizo-affective the sanest. They are caused by imbalances in the blood system in turn caused by faulty adrenals, a discovery made by Folsom in 2009 which brought about effective drug therapy which wholly wiped this scourge from mankind by 2035. We are no longer a schizoid race. We have made great advances over these centuries. Our goals are perfectly reasonable: they involve the conquest of the universe.

7.

"Please," the Captain says to me as we slide into orbit, "please think about this; don't you recognize your own symptomatology?" But it is entirely too late for that. I silence the lunatic with a single threatening gesture and then I press the button, fondling it only slightly, the lovely button so resilient in its dimensions and I see the fire, the brilliant arcing fire that shows the bombs glancing off atmosphere into immediate connection and just as I do so, as I accomplish the desired, I feel my will and rigidity collapse like scaffolding and from that instant am as mad as the Captain. I am as mad as the Captain. Feel myself choked by sobs, remorse, pain, guilt, anguish, because I have destroyed the arthopods: the lovely, lovely arthopods, that through their great gift wanted to bring back the sanity we had lost hundreds of years ago and I too stupid to see it. Beside me, still bound, the Captain is mumbling of defense mechanisms. I do not want to think of defense mechanisms but only of the arthopods: those wise and saddened creatures who now (perhaps I am dreaming this) lie as ash beneath us while our little ship, on full automatic, speeds back toward Ganymede to give the joyful news.

and walk now gently through the fire

By R. A. LAFFERTY

1. 

THE ICHTHYANS or Queer Fish are the oddest species to be found in any of the worlds. They are pseudo-human, perhaps, but not android. The sign of the fish is not easily seen on them, and they pass as human whenever they wish: a peculiarity of them is that they often do not wish to pass as human even when their lives depend on it. They have blood in their veins, but an additional serum also. It is only when the organizational sickness is upon them (for these organizing and building proclivities they are sometimes known as the Queer Builders or the Ants of God), that they can really be told from humans. There is also the fact that most of them are very young, or at least of a youthful appearance. Their threat to us is more real than apparent and we tend to minimize it. This we must not do. In our unstructured, destructed, destroyed society, they must be counted as the enemies to be exterminated. It's a double danger they offer us: to fight them on their own grounds, or to neglect to fight them. They'd almost trick us into organizing to hunt down their organization.

"Oh, they can live near as loosely as ourselves in their deception. These builders can abandon buildings in their trickery. They'll live in tents, they'll live in huts, they'll live under the open sky as easily as do ourselves, the regular people. But observe (they trick us there again: observation is a quality of theirs, not of ours), notice that everything they do is structured. There is always something structured about their very tents; there is something peculiarly structured about their huts; they even maintain that there is something structured about the open sky. They are the Institutional People.

"The Queer Fish claim that Gaea (Earth) is the most anciently peopled of the worlds and that they themselves are the most ancient people. But they set their own first appearance in quite late times, and they contradict the true ancientness of humans and proto-humans.

"The Queer Fish have been bloody and warlike in their times. They have been Oceanic as well as Sky-Faring, in some cases beyond ourselves in that phase. They have even been, in several peculiar contexts, creative. They are not now creative in the arts (they do not even recognize the same arts as we do). They are certainly not creative in the one remaining genuine art, that of unstructured music. They are something much worse than creative now: they are procreative in the flesh. Their fishy flesh would have already become dominant if they hadn't been ordered hunted to extinction. Even in this they force us to come out of ourselves, to use one of their own words.

"They force us to play their game. We have to set up certain structures ourselves to effect their destruction. We even need to institute certain movements and establishments to combat their Institutionalism and Establishmentalism. They are, let us put it plainly, the plague-carriers. Shall we, the Proud Champions of the Destroyed Worlds, have to abandon a part of our thesis to bring about their unstructuring, their real destruction? Must we take unseemly means to balk their fishy plague? We must."

Problem of the Queer Fish. Analects.—The Putty Dwarf.

Judy Thatcher was moving upcountry in a cover of cattle. The millions of feral cattle were on all the plains. Most of these cattle were wobble-eyed and unordered. But an ordered person, such as Judy, would have ordered cattle; she could draw them about her like a cloak, whole droves of them. A person with a sense of structure could manipulate whole valleys of these cattle, could turn them (the smaller units turning the larger), could head them any way required, could use them for concealment or protection, could employ their great horned phalanxes as a threat. Judy Thatcher had some hundreds of her own ordered bulls. Being magic (she was one of the Twelve) she could manipulate almost anything whatsoever.

But most of the cattle of the plains were not quite cattle, were not ordered cattle. Most of the horses were not quite horses, nor the dogs dogs. Most of the people were no longer quite people (this from the viewpoint of the Queer Fish; Judy was a Queer Fish).

Judy was a young and handsome woman of rowdy intellect. She had, by special arrangement, two eyes outside of her head, and these now traveled on the two horizons. These eyes were her daughter, traveling now about two miles to the East and right of her on a ridge, and her son moving on another ridge three miles to her left and West. She was a plague carrier, she and hers. All three of them were Queer Fish.

The son, on her West and left, worked along a North-running ridge in those high plains and he could scan the filled plain still farther to the West. He could mark every disordered creature on that plain, and he had also been marking for some time one creature that was wrongly ordered but moving toward him with a purpose.

This son, Gregory, was twelve years old. Being of that age, he knew it was time for a certain encounter. He knew that the creature, wrongly ordered and moving towards him with a purpose, would be a party to that encounter. This always happens to boys of that age, when they are of the ripe time for the Confirmation or the Initiation of whatever sort. Many boys, unstructured boys, amazed boys of the regular species, boys of the Queer Fish even, are not conscious of the encounter when it comes. It may come to them so casually that they miss its import. It may come as wobble-eyed as themselves and they accept it without question. It may even come to them in dream state (whether in waking or walking dream, or in night dream), and then it sinks down, yeasting and festering a little bit but not really remembered, into their dream underlay. But many boys, particularly those of the Queer Fish species, know it consciously when it comes, and they negotiate with it.

(As to the ritual temptation of girls, that is of another matter, and perhaps it is of earlier or later years. Any information must come from a girl, or from a woman who remembers when she was a girl. Many do not seem to remember it at all. Most will deny it. Some will talk around it, but they do not talk of it directly. You may find an exceptional one who will. You may *be* an exceptional one who knows about it. But it isn't in the records.)

Gregory Thatcher, being twelve years old and in his wits, was tempted by a devil on a high spot on that ridge. There had been a cow, a white-eyed or glare-eyed cow, coming blindly towards him. The cow had no order or purpose, but someone in the cow came on purpose. Then the cow was standing, stock-still, blind-still, too stupid to graze, too balkish to collapse, less animate than a stone cow. Whoever had been in her had come out of her now. Where was he?

There was a little flicker of black lightning, a slight snigger, and he was there.

"Command that these stones be made bread," he said (his heart not quite in it). He was a minor devil; his name was Azazel. He wasn't the great one of that name, but one of the numerous nephews. There is an economy of names among the devils.

"Does it always have to start with those same words?" Gregory asked him.

"That's the way the rubric runs, boy," Azazel jibed. "You Fish are strong on rubric yourselves, you're full of it. Play the game."

"We *are* the rubric," Gregory said easily, "in the first meaning, the red meaning. We're the red ocher, the red earth."

"A smart Fish I have, have I? You heard the words 'Command that these stones be made bread.' Do it, or confess that you are unable to do it. You Fish claim powers."

"It is easy enough to make bread *with* these stones," said Gregory. "Even you can see that they are all roughly quern stones, grinding stones. They are all flat or dished limestones and almost any two will fit together. And the wild wheat stands plentiful and in full head. It's easy enough to thresh it out by rubbing the ears in my hands, to grind it to meal or to flour between your stones, to mix with water from my flask and salt from my pack, to build a fire of cow chips and make bread cakes on one of the flat rocks put to cap the fire. I've dined on this twice today. I'd dine with you on it now if fraternizing were allowed."

"It isn't, Greg. You twist the words. They are 'Command that these stones be made bread,' not 'Command that these stones make bread.' You fail it."

"I fail nothing, Azazel." (The two of them seemed about the same age, but that was not possible.) "You'll not command me to command. On with it, though."

"Cast thyself down from this height," Azazel ordered. "If you are one of the elect you'll not be dashed to pieces by it."

"I'll not be dashed to pieces yet. It's high but not really steep. Not a good selection, Azazel."

"We work with what we are given. The final one then—the world and all that is in it—." Here Azazel went into a dazzle. He was real enough, but now he went into contrived form and became the Argyros Daimon, the Silver Demon who was himself a literary device and diversion. He waved a shimmering silvery hand. "The world and all that is in it, all this I will give you, if—." Then they both had to laugh.

"It isn't much of a world you have to offer," Greg Thatcher grinned. "Really, where is the temptation?"

"No, it doesn't look like much," Azazel grinned. "Oh, the temptation is quite real, but it's subtle and long-term. It's quite likely that you'll be had by it, Greg. Almost all are had by it along the way. You can see it as wheat-colored, or as green-grass colored, or as limestone and dust, or as shimmering. It isn't a simple world, and you haven't seen it all. Already you love it, and you believe you have it. You haven't it yet, not till I give it to you. You're a stranger on it. And you're blind to its main characteristic."

"What characteristic am I blind to?"

"The surface name of it is freedom."

"I have the ordered sort of freedom now," Gregory said rather stiffly. The Odd Fish have always had this somewhat stiff and pompous and superior way of setting forth their views. Whether it is a strength or a weakness is disputed but it is essential to them. They'd not be the Odd Fish without it. "Have you Freedom in Hell?" he asked Azazel. "Have you Order there?"

"Would we offer you something we don't have ourselves?" Azazel asked with his own pomposity. (The Devils and the Odd Fish both have this stilted way of talking, and they have other similarities, but in most ways they are quite different.) "Certainly we have Freedom, the same Freedom that all others have on Earth, the Freedom that you Queer Fish deny yourselves. And Order, here you touch us in a sore spot, Greg. It is here that we offer you a little more than we do have ourselves, for we offer you freedom from order. Aye, regrettably we suffer order of a sort, but you needn't. There's a line in one of the old poets of your own Queer Fish species: 'They order things so damnably in Hell.' He's right, in his way. There is a damnable order still surviving there.

"Let me explain something to you though, Greg. Let me ask you a favor. I'll even appeal to the 'good side' of you. You Queer Fish make much of that 'good side' business. If I am able to disorder you, by that same measure I am allowed to escape into disorder myself. I've made good progress in my time. I've disordered very many. Look not at me like that! You are almost critical of me. I want you. You're a great prize." (The Queer Fish are almost as susceptible to flattery as are the Devils themselves, and Gregory had flushed slightly from pleasure.)

"But I have it all, the world and its fruits," he explained to Azazel. "And I have things that are beyond the world. I walk in light."

"Here's a pair of blued sunglasses you can use then, Greg. The light is always over-bright. You haven't it all. You're afraid of so much of it. I'll take away your fear. All flesh is grass, it is said by some old authority, I forget whether by one of yours or ours. Why do you refuse the more spirited grasses and hemps then? Even the cattle know enough to enjoy them."

"The wobble-eyed cattle and the wobble-eyed people are on the loco. I'll not be on it."

"Come along with our thing, Greg, and we'll help both ourselves into Freedom and Disorder. You can have it the other way also: All grass is flesh. What flesh!"

The things that Azazel demonstrated were fleshy in the extreme. They were like old pictures, but they came on multidimensional and musky and writhing. Wherever the creatures came from white-eyed cows that were not quite cows or out of the ground that was not quite ground Greg did not know. Perhaps they were no more than surrogate projections. What then of those whose lives were no more than surrogate projections, they of the great disordered majority?

"They have so much, Greg," Azazel said, "and you miss it all."

Gregory Thatcher broke the whole complex of devices to pieces with a shattering laugh. It was a nervous laugh though. Gregory had an advantage. He was young, he was only twelve, and he was not precocious. (But from this day on it couldn't be said that he was not precocious. In that complex instant he was older by a year; he was as old as Azazel now.)

"I'll not say 'Get thee behind me, Satan' for I wouldn't trust you behind me for one stride," Gregory laughed. "I will say 'Get thee back into thy cow and be off' for I now perceive that the white-eyed cow there is no cow at all but only a device and vehicle of yours. Into it and be gone, Azazel."

"Greg, boy, think about these things," Azazel spoke as a knowing young fellow to one even younger and not quite so knowing. "You will think about them in any case. I've been talking to you on various levels, and not all my speech has been in words and not all meant to enter by the ears. Parts of it have gone into you by other orifices and they will work in you in your lower parts. Ah, some of those things of mine were quite good. I regret that you refuse the savor of them in your proper consciousness and senses, but they'll be with you forever. We've won it all, Greg. Join it. You don't want to be with the losers."

"You worry and fret as though you'd not quite won it, Azazel," Gregory mocked. "Into your vehicle and be off now. The show wasn't really as well done as I expected."

"The show isn't over with, boy," Azazel said.

There had been a white-eyed cow standing, stock-still, blind-still, too stupid to graze, less animate than a stone cow, an empty cow skin standing uncollapsed.

There had been a teen-aged devil named Azazel, sometimes in a silver dazzle, sometimes in a blue funk, who had talked in words for the ears and in non-words for other entry.

Then there was only one of them. With a laugh, the devil disappeared into the white-eyed cow and she became quite animate. She whistled, she did a little cross-legged dance, she skittered off, blind and bounding. She was full of loco weed as were almost all the creatures of these plains. Aye, and she was full of the devil, too.

And how was one to distinguish an artificial and vehicular cow from a real one? All the cows now looked artificial. They had become like great spotted buffalo in their going feral. They were humpbacked now and huge, wild and wooly, except that they were mostly somnambulistic and stumbling, with an inner pleasure, perhaps, or an inner vacuity.

And the horses of the plains also. What was the tired weirdness about the horses?

And the dogs. However had the dogs become undogged? How is a dog disarticulated?

And the people. They were unpersoned and perverse now. They all shared a secret, and the secret was that they were a shared species with few individuals among them.

Cows, horses, dogs, people, the four artificial species. Now strange contrivances had spouted out of them all and recombined in them. They were all wobble-eyed, white-eyed, vacant-eyed, and freakish.

Except the Queer Fish. The Queer Fish Gregory Thatcher whistled, and the birds whistled and called back to him. How had the birds been spared? Meadow Larks, Scissor Tails, MockingBirds, they all still used structured music.

The Queer Fish Gregory had been noticing movement in the center plains where his mother Judy had been traveling. The movement did not seem to constitute a threat. Some dozen of the ordered bulls of Judy Thatcher had surrounded a creature. They escorted him or it down into the center of the valley; they escorted him with benign throating and bellowing. So it was a visitor to them, and not a hostile visitor. It was possibly one of the Seventy-Two, or one of the looser penumbra. Gregory stood and waited a moment for the signal. It came. The two eyes that Judy Thatcher had outside of her head she called in to her now. Gregory went down into the valley from its West slope. His sister was descending from the opposite rampart.

2.

"We owe so much to one phrase that we can hardly express it. Without it, we'd have had to invent a phrase, we'd have put a modicum of meaning into it (overestimating the intelligence of the people as we have done so many times), and we'd have failed and failed and failed again. One smiles to recall that phrase that our fathers accidentally stumbled on and which later came back to us a hundredfold like bread cast upon the waters: 'I am all for relevant religion that is free and alive and where the action is, but institutional religion turns me off.' Incredible? Yes. A hog, if he could speak, wouldn't make so silly a statement: a blind mole wouldn't. And yet this statement was spoken many millions of times by young human persons of all ages. How lucky that it had been contrived, how mind boggling that it was accepted. It gave us victory without battle and success beyond our dreams.

"It was like saying 'I love animals, all animals, every part of them: it is only their flesh and their bones that I object to; it is only their living substance that turns me off.' For it is essential that religion (that old abomination) if it is to be religion at all (the total psychic experience) must be institutionalized and articulated in organization and service and liturgy and art. That is what religion is. And everything of a structured world, housing and furniture and art and production and transportation and organization and communication and continuity and mutuality is the institutional part of religion. That is what culture is. There can no more be noninstitutional religion than there can be a bodiless body. We abjure the whole business. We're well quit of the old nightmare.

"What was, or rather what would have been, the human species? It was, would have been, the establishment of a certain two-legged animal. This had never been done of any species, and by a very narrow margin it was not done in this case. It would have been Structuring and Organization and Institution erected where such things had never been done before. It would have been the realization of worlds where worlds had not been before. It would have been the building of the 'Sky Bucket' for containing and shaping humanity. And if that 'Sky Bucket' should actually have been built and have been filled to the brim, the human race would have appeared; and it would have been transcendent. The first requirement of the 'Human' is that it should be more than human. Again, we abjure the whole business. We'd rather remain unstructured monkeys.

"Fortunately we have halted it, before critical mass could have been achieved, before even the bottom of the 'Sky Bucket' was covered with the transcendent flowing that might have become human. We have succeeded in unmaking the species before it well appeared. And a thing unmade once is unmade forever, both as to its future and its past. There never was a 'Sky Bucket;' there never was a transcendent flowing; there never was a structured human race or even the real threat of one.

"Our surviving enemies are slight ones, the plague-carrying Queer Fish and others of their bias. We'll have them down also, and then it will be the case that they never were up, that they never were at all. We have already disjointed the majority of them and separated them from their basis. And when they have become disjointed and de-structed and disestablished, they become like ourselves in their co-prophility and in their eruction against order.

"We have won it. We have unmade the species. We have created the case that it has never been. We have carried out our plan to the end that there never need be any sort of plan again. We have followed our logic to its conclusion. The logical conclusion of the de-structing process is illogic. So we had intended it to be. So we have now achieved it."

The Unmaking of the Species. Analities.–The Coprophilous Monkey

The visitor was a long, lean, young man who had been put through the torture. He was close cropped and bare faced and he wore only that day's dirt and dust. He was washing now in the shallow stream. Gregory gave him soap made of bull fat and potash, and he took the visitor's clothes from him for strongest washing.

The visitor had made his request from Judy Thatcher before Gregory's arrival. She had felt a sudden fear at it, but she put it away from her. Now Judy, the mother and magic person, was writing a letter. She wrote on a great flat stone that providentially would serve her for table and desk and for a third function. Why should the stone not serve her providentially? Judy was a child of Providence.

Trumpet Thatcher, the daughter of Judy, the sister of Gregory, had called a horse. This was an ordered horse (there were still a few such), and not one of the wobble-eyed not-quite-horses of the plains. Being an ordered animal, of its nature it obeyed her orders, and she rode it freely across the valley.

"He has not been followed, not closely at least," Judy Thatcher called to her daughter, looking up from her writing. "The danger is not now. The danger is tomorrow, after he has left us a while, when he may fall in with the destructed ones who have followed him (but not closely), when he might bring them, if he is of the treason."

"Nevertheless, I will ride and look," the girl named Trumpet called. And she rode and looked.

The long, lean, young man seemed uneasy at the speculation that he might belong to the treason. He was tired-eyed, but he was not yet truly wobble-eyed. He was wordless and not quite open, but he seemed to have a sanity about him. That he was of the torture meant nothing; he might still be of the treason.

He had been lashed and gashed and burned and broken, that was true. It had been done to him in other years, and it had also been done to him recently, within a week. But had he been burned and gashed and broken for the Faith?

Many of the unstructured persons now tortured themselves or had themselves tortured, sometimes to try to stir their tired sensations, sometimes out of mere boredom. It was a last sensation of those who had sensationalized everything. But the threshold of pain of those tired ones had almost disappeared; the most severe pain would hardly stir them from their drowse. It wasn't the same with them as if an alive and responding person were tortured.

The tired-eyed young man said that he was named Brother Amphirropos. He had come to Judy Thatcher, one of the Twelve, and asked for a Letter. This she could not refuse, even if the giving of it meant her life. She gave the letter now, and perhaps her life, with great sweeps of writing in a rowdy hand out of a rowdy mind. She was a special figure. Two thousand years ago she'd have been a male figure and yet that is not quite correct. The Twelve, in their office, had always been hermaphrodites for God. So was Judy in her special moments.

Yet she wrote with difficulty, for all the free-handed sweep of her writing. There are things hard to write, there are things impossible. She dipped her calamary pen in lampblack and in grace and wrote to somebody or something that might no longer be in existence.

Gregory had cleaned up the visitor and his clothes. The visitor rested on cool stones by the stream. He was wordless, he was almost eyeless, he gave out no confidence at all. It would have been so easy to slay him and bury him there under the cottonwoods and then be off a few quick miles before dark. He had no papers, he had no recommendations. He knew the Sign of the Fish, but there had been something unaccustomed and awkward about his way of giving it.

Gregory had gathered a quantity of wild wheat. He threshed it between the palms of his hands, keeping the good grains, blowing the awns and glumes of chaff away. He threshed a good quantity of it. He ground it between quern stones which were naturally about on the plain, ground it fine to flour for the small bread, and coarse to meal for the large bread. He built a fire of cow chips, put a flat capstone or oven stone over the fire on which to bake the two breads. The small bread (which, however, is larger than the world) he mixed with water only and put it, unsalted and without leaven, on the oven stone. The large, or meal bread, was salted and leavened and kneaded with cow milk, and was then let to rise before it was set on the stone to bake.

Trumpet Thatcher, fine-eyed and proud, returned from her circuit ride. Her good eyes had missed nothing, neither flight of birds nor cloud of dust nor unusual drifting of cattle as far as any of the distant horizons that could be seen from the highest ridges. There was no enemy within three hours' ride of them, none within seven hours' walk, and the stranger, Brother Amphirropos, had come on foot. Or had he come on foot? Trumpet Thatcher, a strong and freckled girl, was now freckled with blood and it was not her own. She took a packet to the stranger.

"It is yours," she said. "You will need it when you leave." It was a small, heavy saddlebag, but she handled it as if it were light. And the stranger went white faced and kept silent.

Trumpet set to work to dig a pit. She was a strong girl, two years older than Gregory, and she dug easily. Also she dug with a queer humor. The pit should have been nearly square but she made it long and narrow. Sometimes she looked at the Stranger-Brother Amphirropos as though measuring him with her eyes, and he became very nervous.

"It is long enough and deep enough," she said after a while. Indeed it was long enough and deep enough to serve as grave for this stranger if it were intended for such. Trumpet put cow chips in the bottom of the pit and set fire to them. Then she put in wood from felled cottonwood and sycamores that lined the stream. It gradually grew to a rousing hot fire.

Judy Thatcher looked up and grinned at the shape of the pit her daughter had made, at the joke she had been playing. And Judy became a little more serious when she observed the shaken appearance of Brother Amphirropos.

"It is time," Judy Thatcher said then. She set her writing to one side of the providential flat rock, that rowdy looping screed on which she had been laboring so seriously. She brought the small bread to the providential rock. She also set out water and wild wine from gone-feral grapes.

"Brother Amphirropos, is there something you should say to me or I to thee, either apart, or before my two?" she asked clearly.

"No," the Stranger-Brother said shortly.

"We begin it then," Judy declared. Her two children and the Stranger-Brother gathered around her. She said ordered words. She did ordered things. She structured, she instituted, she transformed. She and they (including the strange Brother Amphirropos) consumed and consummated. The small bread and the small wine were finished. Judy washed her hands with the small water and then poured it into the porous earth. She returned then, smiling and powerful, to her writing.

Trumpet Thatcher put the large bread on to bake.

Gregory ordered a young bull of six months to come. It came, it nuzzled him, it was an ordered young bull and a friend. It went down before him, on foreknees first as though kneeling to him, but that is the way cattle go down. Then down with its high haunches also and on the ground before him. It rolled its head far back into the bulging of its hump. Gregory and the young bull looked eye to eye. Then Gregory cut its throat with a whetted knife.

They strung the young bull up on a tripod of cottonwood poles. Trumpet understood how to aid in this. Brother Amphirropos didn't quite. He was clumsy and unaccustomed to such labor, but they managed. They skinned the animal down. They cut and separated. They set portions of fat aside. They put large parts of ribs and rump into the burning pit to be seared and roasted.

Trumpet made a frame of poles meanwhile. She cut a great quantity of bull meat into long narrow strips and put them on the pole frame to dry in the wind and the smoke. She did other things with other parts of the animal, set aside in crocks blood that she had drawn and further fat. The great intestine and the stomach she had out and everted. She washed them seven times in the stream, using lime, gypsum, ochre mixed with bone ash (from the bull's own bone), soap, soda, natron, and salt in the water for the seven washings.

The large bread was finished. Trumpet Thatcher brought it to the broad providential stone. They had butter and honey with it. Gregory brought aromatic roasts from the burning pit. They cut and broke and feasted, the four of them. They had cider and small wine. They had milk and cheese. They had blackberries and sand plums and feral grapes. They had sour cider for sauce. They feasted for quite a while.

Two coyotes came and begged and were fed. They could have all the small meat they wanted on the plains, but they loved the big meat that had been roasted.

"Will you be staying the night?" Trumpet Thatcher asked the Stranger-Brother Amphirropos.

"No he will not," Judy the mother answered for the stranger. "He must be gone very soon, as soon as we have finished, and I have finished."

"I'll make him a sling of provender then," Trumpet said. She cut a length of the bull's intestine and knotted it. She took strips of the beef that had been wind-drying and smoke-drying and sizzled them in the fire of the pit. She stuffed the length of intestine with them. She melted fat and poured it in with the meat, added honey and berries and grapes, sealed it with more fat, and knotted it finally with the second knot. It was a twenty pound length.

"Take it with you," Trumpet told him.

"I'll have no need for a great thing like that," the Stranger-Brother protested.

"You may have need," Gregory growled. "The treason cuts both ways. You may have to ride hard and fast when it is accomplished, or when it has failed. You can live on that for a very long time. I doubt if your days will near come to the end of it. Mother, are you not finished yet?"

"Yes, I am finished. It's a short and inept thing, but it may carry its own grace."

This was the letter (it was titled Epistle to the Church of Omaha in Dispersal):

"To you who are scattered and broken, gather again and mend. Rebuild always, and again I say rebuild. Renew the face of the earth. It is a loved face, but now it is covered with the webs of tired spiders.

"We are in a post-catastrophe world, and yet the catastrophes did not happen. There are worse things than catastrophes. There is the surrender of the will before even the catastrophes come. There are worse things than war. There are worse things even than unjust war: unjust peace or crooked peace is worse. To leave life by withdrawal is worse than to leave life by murder. To be bored of the world is worse than to shed all the blood in the world. There are worse things than final Armageddon. Being too tired and wobble-eyed for final combat is worse. There are things worse than lust—the sick surrogates of lust are worse. There are things worse than revolution—the half-revolution, the mere turning away, is worse.

"Know that religion is a repetitious act or it is nothing. The 're' is the holy prefix, since nothing is successful the first time. It must be forever the 're,' the returning, the restructuring, the re-lexion, the reconstitution, the building back from defeat. We will rebuild in the dark and in the light; we will work without ceasing.

"Even our mysterious Maker was the Re-deemer, the re-doomer who wrangles for us a second and better doom, the ransomer, the re-buyer, the re-d-emptor. We are sold and we are ransomed, we are lost and we are found. We are dead and we are re-surrected, which is to say 'surged up again.'

"You ask me about the Parousia, the second coming. This has been asked from the beginning. There was urgent expectation of it in the beginning. Then, in the lifetimes of those first ones, there came a curious satisfaction, as though the coming had been experienced anew, as though it were a constant and almost continuing thing. Perhaps there has been a second coming, and a third, and a three hundredth. Perhaps, as the legend has it, it comes every sabbatical, every seventh year. I do not know. I was not of the chosen at the time of the last sabbatical. We are in the days of a new one, but I know now I will not be alive for *the* day of it.

"Be steadfast. Rebuild, restructure, reinstitute, renew."

X-Dmo. Judy Thatcher (one of the Twelve).

Judy had read the epistle aloud in a clear voice. Now she folded it, sealed it, and gave it to the Stranger-Brother Amphirropos.

"What thou doest do quickly," she said.

"Here is horse," Gregory said, "for your horse that my sister Trumpet killed. It was deception for you to leave your horse a distance apart and come to us on foot. No, worry not. You'll not need saddle or bridle. He is an ordered horse, and we order him to take you where you will. Take up your saddlebag and your bull-gut sling with you and be gone."

The Stranger-Brother mounted horse, took the bag and the sling, looked at them with agonized eyes, almost made as if to speak. But whatever words he had he swallowed in his throat. He turned horse and rode away from them. He carried the letter with him.

3.

"It worries us a little that our victories were too easy, that the world fell down before it had hardly been pushed. We have our results and we should rejoice, but we have them so easily that the salt and the sulphur are missing from our rejoicing. There is a lack of elegance in all that we have accomplished. Elegance, of course, was the first thing of which we deprived the humans, but we rather liked it in the small group that was ourselves. It's gone now. It was only a little extra thing in any case, and our own thesis is that there must be none of these little extra things.

"We intended to have our way in the post-cataclysmic world. We do have our way now and the world has all the predicted marks of the post-cataclysmic world, but the cataclysm did not happen. Since our whole objective was for flatness in all things, perhaps we were wrong to expect grandeur in the execution. Ah, but all the fabled mountains of the world were deflated so easily as to leave us unsatisfied. They were made of empty air, and the air has gone out of them.

"The Queer Fish have the saying that the Mysterious Master and Maker of the Worlds came and walked upon this world in historical time; that he will come again; that, perhaps, he has already come again and again.

"Let us set up the counter saying: that the Mysterious Masters and Unmakers of the Worlds (Ourselves) walk upon this world now; that we diminish it as we walk upon it; that we will not leave a stone upon a stone remaining of it.

"How is a person or a world unmade or unformed? First by being deformed. And following the deforming is the collapsing. The tenuous balance is broken. Insanity is introduced easily under the name of the higher sanity. Then the little candle that is in each head is blown out on the pretext that the great cosmic light can be seen better without it. Then we introduce what we used to call, in our then elegant style, Lady Narkos, Lady Porno, Lady Krotos, Lady Ephialtes, and Lady Hypnos; or Dope, Perversion, Discordant Noise, Nightmare or Bad Trip, and Contrived Listlessness or Sleep. We didn't expect it to work so easily, but it had been ripening for a long while.

"The persons and the worlds were never highly stable. A cross-member is removed here on the pretext of added freedom. Foundation blocks are taken away on the pretext of change. Supporting studs are pulled down on the pretext of new experience. And none of the entities had ever been supported more strongly than was necessary. What happens then? A man collapses, a town, a city, a nation, a world. And it is hardly noticed.

"The cataclysm has been and gone. The cataclysm was the mere gnawing away of critical girders and rafters by those old rodents, ourselves. And who are we? The Queer Fish say that we are unclean spirits. We aren't; perhaps we are unclean materialities. We do not know or care what we are. We are the Unmakers, and we have unmade our own memories with the rest of it. We forget and we are forgotten.

"There was no holocaust, there was no war, there was no predicted overcrowding or nature fouling. The nature fouling came later, from undercrowding. Parts of the cities still stand. Certain diminished black tribes are said still to inhabit their jungles. But, though it has been only thirty years, nobody remembers what the cities really were or who built them.

"We discovered that most persons were automatic, that they operated, as it were, by little winders. One had only to wind them up and they'd say 'That's where the action is, that's where the action is,' and then they'd befoul themselves. And to these little people winders there was always a mechanism release. When tired of playing with the mechanical people, we pushed the release. And the people were then rundown, inoperative, finished."

The Destroying of the World. Aphorisms.—The Jester King.

It was late in the day after the Stranger-Brother had left them.

"Let us flame the fire high," Gregory said, "that they may think we are still here. Then, when full dark comes, let us take horse and ride South to reverse our direction: or better, go West where there has been no show of action."

"I have not been told to go anywhere beyond this place," Judy said doubtfully. "Besides, we do not know for sure that it is the treason."

"Of course it is the treason!" Trumpet Thatcher affirmed. "But I do hope he gets clear of them after he has betrayed you and us. I've never liked their treason that cuts two ways. Why must they always kill the traitor as well as the betrayed? From his eyes, though, I don't believe that he wants to get clear of them."

"What are you waiting for, mother?" Gregory asked.

"For Levi, I think," Judy said doubtfully, dreamily.

"And who is Levi?"

"I really don't know. I believe he is just Levi from over the sea."

"Is there to be a meeting?" Gregory asked. "Are you to be a part of it?"

"There is to be a meeting, I think. I do not believe now that I will be a part of it. I will be dead."

"Well, have you any instructions at all for Trumpet and for myself," Gregory asked, "what we should do?"

"None at all," Judy admitted. "It goes blank. I am out of it soon."

"Should we not at least flame the fires and then move maybe two miles North under the dark?" Gregory asked. "We should not be completely sitting prey."

"All right," Judy said. "We'll go a ways, but not far yet." But she seemed listless as though it had indeed ended with her.

They flamed their fires to mark their old position. They packed meat into slings to carry with them. They burned the remnants of the young bull in the flaming pit then. They moved maybe two miles North. Judy gave instructions to a dozen of the big, horned, ordered bulls. Then Judy and Trumpet bedded down for the night.

Gregory took horse and rode in the night, anywhere, everywhere. As a Queer Fish, Gregory had now come of age on the plains, but he was still a twelve-year-old boy whose personal memory did not go back to any of the great events.

The Day of the Great Copout had been thirty years before. Even Gregory's mother Judy had nothing but scant childhood memories of the days before the Copout. The legends and the facts of that event had now parted company considerably, but it had always been more legend than fact to it. The only fact was that the human race had one day slipped a cog; that it had fallen down from the slight last push, though it had withstood much more severe buffeting. The fact was that the race now built no more and sustained no more, that it had let the whole complexity run down and then looked uncomprehending at the stalled remnant of it.

The legend was that the Day of Freedom arrived for everyone, and that thereafter nobody would ever work at all. The people were very heroic in their refusal to work, and many of them starved for it. Their numbers fought in the cities (always under the now universal peace symbol) for what food and goods could be found there. Their greatly diminished numbers then moved into the countrysides which had for a long time been choked with their sad abundance. Every grain elevator was full to bursting, every feed lot and pasture had its animals to excess. Every haybarn and corncrib was full.

Before the Day of the Great Copout the population had already greatly diminished. In the Americas it was less than a third of what it had been a century before. In other lands it was down variously. The world had already begun to fall apart a bit (being so alike everywhere there was not much use in keeping up communication between the like parts) and to diminish in quality (why run if no one is chasing you?).

But the Day of the Great Copout was worldwide. As though at a given signal (but there had been no signal) people in every city and town and village and countryside of earth dropped their tools and implements and swore that they would work no more. Officials and paper shufflers ceased to officiate and to shuffle paper. Retailers closed up and retailed no more. Distributors no longer distributed. Producers produced nothing. The clock of the people stopped although some had believed that the hour was still early.

The Last Day had been, according to some.

"The Last Day has not been," said a prophet. "They will know it when it has been."

There was a little confusion at first. Though distributors no longer distributed nor retailers retailed, still they objected to their stores and stocks being looted. There was bad feeling and bloodshed over this, and the matter was never settled at all.

The law people had all resigned from the law; and every congress and assembly in the world stood adjourned indefinitely or forever. There were, for a while, new assemblies and gatherings, freely chosen and freely serving, but these quickly fell apart and left nothing in their places but random gangs.

Minorities of odd people resisted the disintegration for a while, becoming more odd and more minor in their exceptions. The Crescent Riders kept up a little order for some years in the older parts of the world, not really laboring, looting just enough that the art be not forgotten; still keeping leaders who looked a little like leaders. The Ruddy Raiders maintained that there was nothing wrong with rape and arson so long as it was done as fun and not labor. The Redwinged Blackbirds and the Mandarins held together here and there.

And among certain groups that had always been considered peculiar, The Witnesses, the Maccabees, the Queer Fish, the Copout had not been complete. Certain numbers of these folks, somewhere between five and ten percent of them, resisted the Freakout, the Copout, the Freedom Day. These minorities of minorities had the compulsion to continue with their building, their ordering, their planting, creating, procreating.

This caused a disturbance in the New Free World. Groups should not be free to reject Free Think. So these remnants were hunted down. Even though it was against the new ways of the Free World, a certain organization was necessary for the hunts.

Most of that had passed now. Most of everything had passed. After thirty years had rolled by, the Free People of the world had become pretty old, pretty old and pretty crabby. Though most of the males among them still wore the beards of their boyhood and youth, yet they had aged in every way. They hadn't been reproducing themselves to any great extent; and the most of them hadn't really been so very young when the Great Day had come and gone. The cult of youth had become a bit senile.

There were still some populations in the cities. The cities have always been built on the best lands of the country and have always occupied the best river bottoms and river junctions. There was good fishing, there was good grazing on the new grass that shattered the pavements and sidewalks, on the open places which became still more open, there was good fuel of several sorts, there were buildings remaining that were still tight enough to give year-round protection.

But most of the folks were in the countrysides now. The special grasses and hemps and poppies necessary to the Free Culture had long been established and abundant; they were in the cities and the countries and the fringe areas. In the country were millions upon millions of now feral-cattle to be had for easy killing. Wheat and corn still grew of themselves, rougher and more ragged every year, but still more than sufficient. The scattered crops would apparently outlast the diminished people, the disappearing human race.

What children and young people there were now belonged, much beyond their expected percentages, to the peculiar groups. Children of the regular people also showed some tendency to join these peculiar groups. It was almost the case that any young person was now suspect. It was quite rare that any young one should really adhere to the Free People. There had even come the anomalous situation (to one who remembered the earlier days and the earlier slogans) that beards were now more typical of old men than of boys.

Such was the world. So had it been for thirty years, for the Freedom Era.

"But there is always hope," Judy Thatcher (and John Thatcher before her) used to preach. "Never has there been so much room for hope, never so great a vacuum waiting to be filled by it. Hope is a substance that will fill a vessel of any shape, even the convoluted emptiness that is the present shape of the world."

"And now in the sabbatical year" (this was Judy Thatcher alone preaching now, for John Thatcher was dead before sabbatical year rolled around) "there is more room for hope than ever before. There are still the Twelve (we have the Word that we will not diminish below that); there are still the further seventy-two traveling and laboring and building somewhere; and there are still the scattered hundreds who will not let it die. Oh, there will be a great new blooming! It begins! It begins!"

"Where? Where does it begin?" Gregory and Trumpet used to ask this rowdy-minded mother of theirs with laughing irony. "Where does it begin at all?"

"With the two of you," Judy would say. "With the dozens, with the hundreds, with the thousands of others."

"Knock off the last zero, mother," Trumpet would always laugh. "There are a few hundreds, perhaps, very widely scattered. But you know there are not thousands."

"There have been thousands and millions," Judy always insisted. "And there will be thousands and millions again."

The Thatchers had been moving for all these years North and South in the marginal land that is a little to the West of the land of really adequate rain. There was plenty here for small bands. The Thatchers and their friends knew all the streams and pools and dry runs where one could dig to water. They had their own grain that seemed to follow their paths and seasons with its own rough sowing. They had their own cattle that were devoted to them in a strangely developed way.

Gregory Thatcher, as the summer starred night was rolling overhead (they were quite a ways North), was remembering the murder of his own father, John Thatcher, two years before. It had been a nervous night like this one, following a daytime visit of a man with not-quite-right eyes, a man with the slight tang of treason on him.

But the man had asked for a letter to take to one of the churches in dispersal. This was given; it could not be refused. And it was given under John Thatcher's own name. The man had also asked for the sacrament; that could never be refused. And the man had been allowed to depart in peace and on foot as he had come. On foot—but a thousand yards away and he was on horse and gone in the afternoon's dust to meet a scheming group.

The group had come just at next dawn, after such a nervous night as this one; had come from an unexpected direction and killed John Thatcher in one swoop. They then were all away except the several who were tossed and killed on the horns of the ordered bulls.

And the stunned reaction had found voice and words only in Judy's puzzled lament:

"It is broken now. There are no longer the full Twelve. It was never supposed to be broken."

"Bend down, woman," dead Thatcher said. "I am not quite dead. I lay my hands on you." John Thatcher laid his hands on his wife Judy and made her one of the Twelve. Then he died (for the second time, Gregory believed. Gregory was sure his father had been killed by first assault, and had come alive for a moment to accomplish what he had forgotten).

"It is all right then," Judy Thatcher had said. "We are still the Twelve. I make the twelfth. I was wrong ever to doubt of that; I was wrong ever to doubt of anything."

So they had buried John Thatcher, the father and still a young man, and rejoiced that the Twelve still survived. That had been two years ago.

Gregory rode his circuit all night. It was his to do. It was not for his mother Judy or for his sister Trumpet. They had other roles. This was Gregory's night. It had a name which he did not know. It was the Watch Night, the night of squires on the eve of their knighting, of princes on the nocturne of their crowning, of apostles on the vigil of their appointing.

There was a nervousness among the cattle here, and again there. There might be several strange bands in motion. The Thatchers had no firearms, no weapons at all that could not be excused or justified as being tools. A few of the roving gangs still had rifles, but these were sorry things near as dangerous to raider as to victim. All such things were thirty or more years old, and none had been well cared for. But the raiders always had bludgeons and knives.

Gregory fell asleep on horseback just before dawn. This was not a violation of the Watch Night for him. It was the one thing for which he never felt guilt. Actually he was cast into deep sleep; it was done to him; it was not of his own doing or failing at all. His horse also was cast into deep sleep, standing, with head bowed down and muzzle into the stiff grass. They both slept like wind-ruffled statues.

Then there was movement, double movement, intruded into that sleep. There was the stirring and arraying of the ordered bulls. There was the false attack; and the bulls went for the false attack, being faithful beasts only.

Then there was the death attack, coming apparently from the West. Gregory himself was struck from his horse. One of the raiders had counted coup on him, but not death coup. He was on the ground begrimed with his own blood and his horse was dead.

Then he heard the clear ringing voice from which his sister had her name. It rose to a happy battle cry and was cut off in quick death. The last note of the Trumpet was a gay one, though. This had been a big happy girl, as rowdy in mien and mind as her mother.

Trumpet Thatcher was dead on the ground: and the mother Judy Thatcher was dead beyond all doubt. There was confusion all around, but there was no confusion about this fact.

The ordered horned bulls had wheeled now on the real attackers. They wrecked them. They tossed them, men and horses, into the air, and ripped and burst them before they came to ground. And the only words that Gregory could find were the same words that his mother Judy had found two years before.

"It is broken now. They are no longer the full Twelve. It was never supposed to be broken."

His mother was quite dead and she would not come alive even for a moment to accomplish what she had forgotten. This dead Thatcher was *not* able to say, "Bend down, boy. I am not quite dead." She *was* quite dead. She would speak no more, her broken mouth would be reconstituted no more, till resurrection morning.

"Are there no hands?" Gregory cried out, dry-eyed and wretched. "Are there no hands that might be laid upon me?"

"Aye, boy, mine are the hands," came a voice. A man of mature years was walking through the arrayed bulls. And they, who had been killing strange men in the air and on the ground, opened their array and let this still stranger man come through. They bowed horns down to the turf to this man.

"You are Levi," Gregory said.
"I am Levi," the man answered softly. He laid hands on Gregory. "Now you are one of the Twelve," he said.

4.

"There has been a long series of 'Arrow Men' or 'Beshot Men' who have been called (or who have called themselves) Sons of God. These Comet-like Men have all been exceptional in their brief periods. The Queer Fish, however, insist that their own particular Mentor 'The Mysterious Master and Maker of the Worlds' was unique and apart and beyond the other Arrow Men or Comet Men who have been called Sons of God. They state that he is more than Son of God: that He is God the Son.

"We do not acknowledge this uniqueness, but we do acknowledge the splendor and destroying brilliance of all these Arrow Men. To us, there is nothing wrong with the term Son of God. There is not even anything wrong with the term God, so long as it is understood to be meaningless, so long as we take him to be an unstructured God. Our own splendor would have been less if there had not been some huge thing there which we unstructured. This unstructuring of God, which we have accomplished, was the greatest masterwork of man.

"The second greatest masterwork of man was the unstructuring of man himself, the ceasing to be man, the going into the hole and pulling the hole in after him; and the unstructuring, the destroying of the very hole then.

"We were, perhaps, the discredited cousins of man. We are not sure now what we were or are. We who were made of fire were asked to serve and salute those who were made of clay. We had been Arrow Men ourselves. Our flight was long flaming and downward, and now it has come to an end. We destroy ourselves also. We'll be no more. It is the Being that we have always objected to.

"The collapsing of the human species was a puzzle for the anthropologists and the biologists, but both are gone now. They said though, before their going, that it is a common thing for a new species to collapse and disappear; that the collapse, in these common cases, is always sudden and complete; they said that it was an uncommon case for any species to endure. They said also that there was never anything unusual in the human species.

"They were almost wrong in this evaluation. There was, or there very nearly was, something unusual about the human species. It was necessary that we alter and tilt things a bit to remove that unusualness. We have done that. We've blown it all for them and for ourselves.

"Fly-blown brains and fly-flown flesh! What, have you not lusted for rotted mind and for rotted meat? Here are aphrodisiacs to aid you. Have you not lusted for unconsciousness and oblivion? You can have them both, so long as you accept them as rotted, which is the same as disordered, or unstructured, or uninstituted. This is the peaceful end of it all: the disordering, the disintegrating, the unstructuring, the rotting, the dry rot which is without issue, the nightmare which is the name of sleep without structure. Lust and lust again for this end! We offer you, while it is necessary, the means and the aids to it."

Mind-Blowing and World-Blowing. Aphrodisiacs.—Argyros Daimon.

(No, really we don't know why these Unstructured Scriveners chose such oddities for calamary names.)

Levi and Gregory were walking northward at a great easy amble. "It is no use to be bothered with horses and so be slowed," Levi said. They moved without hurry but at unusual speed. It was a good trick. Gregory would not have been able to do it of himself, but with Levi he could do it. Levi had a magic way of delving in the earth, as for the two burials. He had this magic way of moving over the earth.

"You are Levi from over the sea," Gregory said once as they moved along over the stiff grass pastures, "but how have you come? There are no longer any planes. There are no longer any ships. Nobody comes or goes. How have you done it?"

"Why Gregory, the world has not slumbered as deeply as you had believed. Things have not ceased completely to be done. Anything can be builded again, or builded a first time. And there are no limits to what a body can do when infused with spirit. Perhaps I walked on the water. Perhaps I traveled for three days in the belly of a whale and he brought me all this way and vomited me up on these high plains. Or perhaps I came by a different vehicle entirely. Oh, is it not a wonderful world that we walk this morning, Gregory!" They were in the dusty Dakota country, coming into that painted and barren region that is called the Bad Lands. Well, it was wonderful to the eye, perhaps, but it was dry and sterile.

"My father and my mother, both gone in blood now, have said that the world has gone to wrack and ruin," Gregory was speaking with some difficulty, "and that there is nothing left but to trust in God."

"Aye, and I say that we can build wonderful things out of that wrack and ruin, Gregory. Do you not know that all the pieces of the world are still here and that many of them are still useable? Know that the world has been not dead but sleeping. 'Twas a foolish little nodding off, but we come awake again now. And this Trust is a reciprocal thing. We must trust in God, yes. And He must trust in us a little. We *are* the Twelve. He puzzles a bit now I think. 'How are they going to get out of this one?' He wonders. Yes boy, I jest, but so does the Lord sometimes. He jests, He jokes, and we be the point of His most pointed jokes. An old sage once said that there were only twelve jokes in the world. What if we be those twelve? The possible humor and richness of this idea will grow in you, Greg, when you meet the others of the Twelve. There are some sly jokes among the pack of us, I assure you of that."

"When will we meet others?" Gregory asked.

"Oh, almost immediately now. It is a new day and a new year and a new rebuilding; we'll set about it almost at once, Greg."

"The regular people have hunted us down like the lowest animals," Gregory vented some of his old feelings. "They say that we are the plague carriers."

"It is life that you carry, Greg, and life is the plague to their wobble-eyed view. But they are no great thing, boy. They are only the Manichees returned to the world for a while, those people who were born old and tired. They are the ungenerating generation and their thing always passes."

"In my life it has shown no sign of passing."

"Your life has been a short one, boy Greg. But I shouldn't call you 'boy'; you are one of the Twelve now. Ah, those sterile parasites have always had a good press though, as the phrase used to be—the Manichees, the Albigenses, the Cathari, the Troubadors (they of the unstructured noise who couldn't carry a tune in a bucket, they in particular have had a good press), the Bogomils, parasites all, and parasites upon parasites. But the great rooted plant survives, and the parasites begin to die now."

"They have spirits also who work for them, Levi," Gregory said. "They have the Putty Dwarf, the Jester King, the Silvery Demon, others."

"Those are parasites also, Gregory. They are mean and noisome parasites on real Devildom, just as their counterparts are parasites on humanity. Listen now to the ordered birds, Gregory, and remember that each of us is worth many birds. It bothered the disordered brotherhoods more than anything that the birds still used structured music. It bothered them in Languedoc, and in Bosnia, and in the Persia of Shapur. It bothered them in Africa, and on these very plains, and it bothers them in hell. Let them be bothered then! They are the tares in the wheat, the anti-lifers."

Gregory Thatcher and Levi Cain had been going along at a great easy ramble, moving without hurry but at unusual speed. But a third man was with them now, and Gregory could not say how long he had been with them.

"You are Jim Alpha," Gregory said (he began to have the magic or insight that his mother had had, that his father had had before her), "and you also come from oversea, from over a slightly different sea than that of Levi."

"I am Jim Alpha, yes, and I have crossed a slightly different sea. We gather now, Gregory. There will be the full set of us, and the secondary set, and also the hundreds. And besides ourselves there will be the Other Sheep. Do not be startled by their presence. They also are under the blessing."

"There are bees in the air. Many thousands of bees," Gregory was saying. "I have never seen so many."

"They are bringing the wax," Jim Alpha was saying, "and a little honey also. No, I don't believe I've ever seen so many of them, not even in sabbatical year. Perhaps this is jubilee also. The bees are the most building and structuring of all creatures, and they have one primacy. They were the first creatures to adore; this was on the day before man was made. It won't be forgotten of them."

Other things and persons were gathering now, thousands of things, hundreds of persons. There was a remembered quality to many of them. "The remembered quality, the sense of something seen before, is only rightness recognized, Gregory," Tom Culpa was saying in answer to Gregory's thought. Tom Culpa must be rightness recognized then, since he was a remembered quality to Gregory Thatcher, he was someone appearing as seen and known before though the thing was impossible. How did Gregory even know his name without being told? Or the names of the others?

There was something coming on that would climax quickly. It was evening, but it was white evening: it would be white night, and then it would be morning. And the inner gathering seemed almost complete.

To Levi and Gregory and Jim Alpha had now gathered Matty Miracle (he was a fat old man; it was a miracle that he could be moving along with them so easily, matching their rapid amble), and Simon Canon, Melchisedech Rioga (what an all-hued man he was!—what was he, Gael, Galla, Galatian, Galilean?), Tom Culpa whose name meant Tom Twin, Philip Marcach, Joanie Gromova (Daughter of Thunder her name meant: Judy Thatcher hadn't been the only woman among the Twelve), James Mollnir, Andy Johnson, and his younger brother Peter Johnson.

"It counts to twelve of us now," Gregory Thatcher said very sagely, "and that means—"

"—that we have arrived to where we were going," Peter Johnson laughed. This Peter Johnson was very young. "Most of the seventy-two are here also," he continued. "Yes, now I see that they are all here. And many of the hundreds. We can never say whether all the hundreds are here."

"Peter," Gregory tried to phrase something a little less than a warning. "There are others here whom we know in a way but do not know by name, who are not of the Twelve nor of the Seventy-Two nor of the Hundreds."

"Oh, many of the Other Sheep are here," Peter Johnson said. "You remember that He said He had Other Sheep?"

"Yes," Gregory answered. He remembered it now. The puzzle was that this Peter Johnson was a boy no older than Gregory. There were many older men there, Levi, Jim Alpha, Matty Miracle, Simon Canon. How was it that Peter Johnson, that other twelve-year-old boy, was accepted as the Prince of them all?

The candle molders were busy. Candle molders? Yes, ten at least of them were working away there, or ten thousand. And full ten thousand bees brought wax to each of them. There would be very many candles burning through the white evening and the white night and on into the white dawn. Then these weren't ordinary candle molders or ordinary bees? No, no, they were the extraordinary of both; they had reality clinging to them in globs of light. Events gathered into constellations.

One using words wrongly or in their usual way might say that everything had taken on a dreamlike quality. No, but it had all lost its old nightmarish quality. It had all taken on, not a dreamlike quality, but the quality of reality.

There was, of course, the acre of fire, the field of fire. This acre was large enough to contain all that needed to be contained: it is always there, wherever reality is. There are tides that come and go; but even the lowest ebbing may not mean the end of the world. And then there are the times and tides of clarity, the jubilees, the sabbaticals. There is reassurance given. The world turns in its sleep, and parts of the world have moments of wakefulness.

Ten million bees had not brought all the wax for that acre of fire, and yet it was a very carefully structured fire in every tongue and flame of it. It was the benevolent illumination and fire of reality. It was all very clear, for being in the middle of a mystery. White night turned into white dawn; and the people all moved easily into the fire, their pomposities forgiven, their eyes open.

The Mysterious Master and Maker of the Worlds came again and walked upon this world in that Moment. He often does so. The Moment is recurring but undivided.

No, we do not say that it was Final Morning. We are not out of it so easily as that. But the moment is all one. Pleasantly into the fire that is the reality then! It will sustain through all the lean times of flimsiness before and after.

the gift of nothing

By JOAN C. HOLLY

MARTIN SUNBEAR scrambled to his feet at the sound of crackling underbrush. Birds shrieked as shouts broke the green Kana silence. It was Hayden's voice, loud and out of breath. Martin leaped the brook that curled through the glen, and ran to meet the voice.

The bushes parted and Tiva ran toward him, her tanned arms outstretched, cradling a small animal. The same sun that made highlights in her black hair glinted in the tears on her cheeks. She stopped, looking at Martin with her black eyes unbelieving.

Hayden, the crew's medic, came behind her, blond and red-faced, his mouth open to shout, but Martin motioned him down. As Alien Contact Officer for the Wasp, he had the right of way in emergencies with Kana's natives, and from the distress of the girl's face, this was an emergency. He glanced at the animal. It was brown and soft furred, the closest thing to a rabbit Kana spawned. Its head and feet hung limply over Tiva's arm. It was dead.

"He killed it," Tiva whispered. "It was running, and he killed it."

They were simple words. Simple enough for Martin to understand without the Translator hookup to the ship's language computer. But he would have known, anyway, from the hurt in her voice and the charred hole in the animal.

Hayden couldn't hold back any longer. "What the hell, it's just a rabbit. She wouldn't listen to reason. She picked it up and started running."

"Did you touch *her?*" Martin demanded.

"No! I followed the prissy rules."

Martin took the animal and laid it gently on the grass. Then he stood staring at it because he didn't know what else to do. Finally he said, "Get a Translator hookup, Hayden. I may need it."

"Why?" Hayden bridled. "It's just a rabbit. It's not that important. Just a woman's idea of pity. You don't need a hookup, anyway. You're fluent."

Martin bit his lip and agreed. Tuned to the language-computer on the *Wasp,* the speaker-transmitter hookup helped whenever a conversation demanded more fluency than any of the crew possessed. But he seldom needed it anymore. He had "taught" the computer at first and then learned from it as fast as it could extrapolate. He was fluent. The other crew members rarely bothered to study the alien language out of their own laziness and their confidence that he would do it.

With communication easier they had all thought their job would be a snap, but something had been wrong about this planet from the start. Since the *Wasp* had first set down two months ago and radioed her safe landing to the mother-ship, *Astra,* Martin had felt a queerness in his stomach. But he could never catch it close enough to examine. More than anything else, it felt like nostalgia—like homesickness—and that was ridiculous.

Meeting the natives and being accepted was almost too easy. The people of Kana were gentle people—kind, happy, and religious. They wore flowers and feathers in their hair and laughed a lot. Brandon, captain of the *Wasp,* called them children. Martin didn't know. They lived as a Stage Four culture should live—in villages of about fifty families, in shelters made of natural materials, with primitive utensils and primitive ceremonies. Beneath their feet was gold, uranium, oil and iron. Around them was an Eden-like world of rich land, clear water and tall forests. There were no carnivores, and the Kanans were vegetarians. They knew life's worth and were contented. But they were unaware that with the descent of the *Wasp,* their world had changed, and they might lose their future.

Tiva stood beside him now, her dark eyes pitiful. He asked her without the hookup, "Tell me what happened, Tiva—please. What made you cry?"

She pointed to the dead animal. "He killed it. I tried to stop him, but he killed it. How could he do that? How could he stand it?"

Hayden shrugged away in disgust, understanding only a bit of what was said.

Martin probed gently, "You are crying for the animal?" He hoped that was all it was. Seeing Hayden running behind her had given him a start. Tiva was too pretty, and there had been one "incident" already.

But she nodded, "Yes. For its spirit. For its freedom and its life. He killed it."

"Is she going to make a big thing out of this?" Hayden fumed. "Can't you make her see it's only a rabbit?"

Tiva turned on him, responding to his tone of voice even though she didn't understand his actual words. She demanded in her own language, "You took this life. What right did you have? Can you make it walk again?"

Hayden swiveled away from her accusing eyes. "What's she talking about, Sunbear?"

"She's trying to tell you what I've said all along. These people don't think anyone has the right to kill. In other words, it's the fifth commandment taken seriously; Thou shalt not kill—period. No specifications. Just, Thou shalt not kill. You knew better."

"I didn't think you meant rabbits."

"I meant *insects,*" Martin answered, then sighed, "You go back to the *Wasp* and leave us alone. I'll try to make her understand."

Hayden left without argument, and Martin began the task of making Tiva see that different people have different values; that, to Hayden, an animal was not equal in life. He had to repeat and repeat to dispel the disbelief on her face. And somehow, telling her made him a little sick. It went against something he'd thought he buried long ago—an inherited resentment that had no place in the modern age.

But he had to make her forgive the mistake. As the daughter of

Chantuka, principle chief of Kana, her feelings carried weight. The old man was walking the edge, swaying between accepting or rejecting their treaty. She could push him to the "no" side.

So he stood in the glade and talked hesitantly in a language that was still only half-learned until he saw her waver and heard her forgive. As an Alien Contact Officer, he knew his trade. But this was the first time he had felt it to be a trade of traitors.

The fire glowed with yellow cracklings and sent shadows jumping into the night and onto the faces of the people circled around it. Two of the four crewmen, Hayden and Lyler, were on one side of the circle with some young native men, and Martin sat on Chantuka's left, Captain Brandon beside him and the missionary, Mr. Evers, next to Brandon. Martin's sole duty was to translate what Brandon was telling the chief about the benefits of a treaty with the other worlds in his attempt to convince the old man to agree to it.

Evers was saying nothing on this particular night. He'd had his innings against Chantuka's god off and on for two months. Tonight he simply listened, his thin, gentle face interested, but calm.

Brandon was a different matter. He was intent and anxious as he filled the old man's head full of the wonders the Kanans would receive in return for permission to establish colonial and mining settlements, listing gifts of plows and tractors for their agricultural economy, medicines, and new knowledge that would boost them overnight from primitive to civilized.

Chantuka remained dignified and quiet, his head tilted toward Martin's translations only slightly, as though the sound was not welcome, just inevitable. He listened and weighed, but never answered.

Brandon tried a new approach, bringing things down to examples so Chantuka could understand. The big, brown-haired, immaculate captain creased his brow and pretended he was talking to a child.

"You've seen our flying machine, Chantuka," he said. "We need materials to feed that machine and all the others like it. Those things you have, underground, deep in your world. If you give permission, my people will come here and dig for them, and in return for your kindness, we will pay you in fine new gifts. Your people will have a new life opened to them. They can be rich and proud. The settlers will come, too, and you'll have new friends, new teachers, new brothers."

As Martin translated, Chantuka remained silent. Only the deepening of his wrinkles showed that he had heard. The firelight glistened in his white hair, and Martin thought there was nothing stern in his face. His life had been too simple for that. Instead, there was wisdom. But Brandon couldn't see it.

Martin was comfortable near Chantuka. The nostalgia disappeared in the chief's presence and he felt at home. But that, too, was ridiculous.

He had never really had a home. He had never belonged anywhere. Somehow the culture of his civilization hadn't gotten through to him. He knew the rules and followed them, but there was some tremendous ingredient lacking. Other people were happy and fulfilled. He was not. He had no roots—no rapport with any of it.

Sometimes when he was on Earth and could attend a monthly chapter meeting of the United Indian Nation, and sit with his own kind in the dim light of a lodgefire and listen to the drums beating rhythms that echoed in the heart and the blood—sometimes, then, he felt at home. But those meetings were few, and when they ended it always meant returning to the bright light of the city waiting outside, watching the feathers being put carefully away and the proper modern street dress slipped back on bodies that for a few hours had been transported backwards in time to another age, another culture.

He often hated the UIN meetings simply because they had to end. Yet he was grateful that his people had managed to increase themselves, take their place in the predominant society so that they could live, and then in a great needing-of-each-other, create and give life to the UIN that preserved the best things from their old ways. Their Indian heritage was strong in all of them and not to be given up, although it made them still suspect among the rest of society, still open to prejudice here and there.

But many times he'd thought that the heritage wasn't as strong in most as it was in himself. The others left the UIN meetings with a quicker step than he, more willing to reenter the outside world, and their attitude only heightened his own resentment. The old ways could never really "be" again, but he had to consciously force himself to accept that fact.

He had wondered if he belonged somewhere else—if there might be a place where he could find the fulfillment other people found—perhaps on some other world. But the search among the stars hadn't provided that place. He was a man between. And the necessary study of history and myriad cultures in order to become an Alien Contact Officer had only deepened his loneliness.

Yet, Kana had an odd effect on him. The Kanans were strangely familiar, not only in their echoing of the copper-bronze of his skin and the black of his hair. It was more. They touched the same spirit in him that the old, lost culture stirred to life. But if Kana turned out to be "his" place in the universe, how could he keep it? With the coming of missionaries, miners, and colonizers, Kana would become one more link in the chain of Earth's society. And then the door would close and he would again have no home. Here, by Chantuka, he could at least pretend for a while.

But Brandon continued to rupture the mood. He switched to English entirely and spoke gruffly. "You're not giving me much help, Sunbear. These people are tame enough. Why won't they come through?"

"Maybe they're too tame," Martin answered, not sure, himself, what he really meant. "Anyway, persuading them isn't my job."

"But I get the feeling you're pulling the other way. I think the old man senses it, too. He likes you, and he'll trust your judgment." Brandon leaned closer. "We've got to have this planet. It's the richest strike in years. Land—ore—forests—. Lyler's got his first mineral estimates finished and he says it's fantastic. There shouldn't be any problem. We've made treaties with people worse than cannibals. Where's the trouble?"

Martin shifted, reluctant to answer. "I think it's a matter of philosophy. Religion, if you like. These people aren't cannibals. They're not like any people we've met. They're an old, old race."

"And pagan," said Evers, the expedition's missionary.

Martin glanced at him, keeping his face expessionless. He couldn't argue with Evers. The missionary was a man with decent intentions. One missionary accompanied each scouting trip to begin the conversion of the people to Standard Christianity—the Standard Faith —and to protect the natives, when possible, from the harsher realities of alien contact. At least that was what they "thought" they were doing. Martin often had his own ideas.

Brandon said, "They haven't progressed one iota in who knows how many years. They're stuck in some backward time slot."

"They're happy," Martin answered. "Why should they change?"

"Happy, perhaps," Evers inserted his voice again, "but certainly not striving toward the proper morality, not obeying the only true God. I have to agree with Captain Brandon. They're caught in a backward time slot. I'm not really interested in the crusade for a treaty, Martin. You know that. I only want to bring these people into God's fold."

Martin read the sincerity on the man's face. But Evers, too, didn't look beyond his personal view to the result of what he wanted to do on Kana. He and Brandon were working from different starting points, but heading for the same locus—colonization, change, and to Martin's mind—ruin. He wasn't even certain why he felt the coming ruin so strongly in the pit of his stomach. He had helped to make treaties with other worlds and had never sensed this reluctance in himself before.

"They need us," Brandon insisted. "Look what we can do for them." Martin could almost taste the Captain's frustration. Brandon believed that no one could be truly happy without the things that made *him* happy. He had things in his hands to give the Kanans, but Chantuka refused to accept them. "What I need is something tangible I can use to prove my point. Something dramatic, maybe. Think about it, Sunbear. We don't have much time. The *Astra* will be leaving this system in three weeks and I have to take this planet back with me. Peacefully."

"All I can give you is a word of warning," Martin scowled across the circle where Hayden and Lyler were teaching some young men to shoot craps. "Keep the crew in line. Don't let another incident occur. And stop treating Chantuka like a child. Be careful what you say because he believes every word. He doesn't know about stretching the truth."

Brandon stared at him hard, trying to see the emotion behind his words. Brandon had sensed that something about him didn't ring true anymore. "Your feathers starting to show, Sunbear? You think only savages can be honest?"

Martin let the snide remark pass as he always did. Bigotry, it seemed, had an eternal life of its own.

When he got no response to his baited stab, Brandon straightened and made his tone official. "Three more weeks is all the time we have. When that's up, we've got to have a treaty."

Martin tightened his jaw. He understood. Men in the Scouting Service never failed because the alternative was too grave for both sides. When a suitable planet was found, it was taken, "suitable" meaning only that it was habitable and held no biological danger. Biological quarantine was the *only* exception. If the planet wasn't raped by treaty, it was raped by force, and when it came to violence, both natives and invaders died.

Chantuka would decide it all for Kana, and as much as he ached to, Martin wasn't allowed to tell him that his choice was really between agreement or invasion.

Evers cleared his throat and offered, "Perhaps if I keep trying, captain. Let me go on talking to Chantuka about God and the new Path that I can teach his people. He listens when I talk. I may be able to persuade him to your treaty by making him want religion."

"*Our* religion," Martin muttered. "Our hodgepodge."

"What does hodgepodge mean?" Evers challenged him. His eyes were sharper now, his gentleness less apparent.

"Forget it," Martin said, then reversed himself and spoke his mind. "What else can you call taking every organized religion that existed on Earth and incorporating them all into one? And then even adding dogma from some other powerful cultures we've met just to get them to go along with us more willingly?"

Evers' voice chilled, "You think I preach hodgepodge? How were you raised, Martin Sunbear? Weren't you instructed in the Standard Faith?"

Martin shrugged. He didn't want to admit another personal difference to set him still further apart. But he wouldn't lie, either. "I was instructed in the Standard Faith. But my parents also taught me Christianity."

"The old, narrow Christianity?"

Martin admitted it. "According to that 'obsolete' book called the Bible. Yes."

Brandon guffawed. "You redskins never could stick to the law, could you? I'll bet that bible was well laced with chants and spirit dances. Incredible!"

Martin suddenly wanted to confess to that accusation, too; he suddenly wanted to get it all out as he had never done before. He *had* been taught the rudiments of the ancient tribal beliefs, and he had gone further, haunting libraries and studying it for himself. But those facts weren't for Brandon's ears.

He sighed, sure he should have kept his mouth closed in the first place. He was only here as an interpreter tonight. And he had to stem the disagreement before it could turn into an argument because he noticed that Chantuka was leaning closer, gazing steadily at their faces, anxious to understand their conversation even though he only knew a word or two of their language.

"Forgive me for saying anything, Mr. Evers," Martin apologized. "I don't usually interfere."

"No, I guess not!" Brandon said. "You're usually the stoic all the way around. I've always figured you needed watching."

It was a direct challenge, but Martin couldn't take it up. "Please, let's not go on with this because certain parties shouldn't hear us quarrel," he warned. "Tone of voice is as understandable as actual words."

Evers and Brandon followed his glance to Chantuka, realized his meaning, and immediately resumed their former relaxed postures. Evers jumped right back to what he had been telling Brandon before, as though nothing had come between. "I still believe it would be the best course, captain. Let *me* talk to the old man. In my own time. I can convince him that our way is what God wants of him."

Martin thought bitterly to himself, "*Scare* him into believing it, you mean." He didn't voice it.

"All right," Brandon agreed. "Talk. I'll lay off a week on you, preacher, but no more. I can't change any more than that."

Another week passed as Mr. Evers huddled with Chantuka, pressing into his ears stories of how God was vengeful and angry when people didn't follow His appointed ways once they had learned about Him from the proper source.

Evers was becoming decently proficient in the Kanan language, himself, and with the use of a computer hookup, had little need of Martin, so Martin gratefully left the constant talks, a foul taste in his mouth that came from translating words *he* didn't believe for the benefit of an old and wise native who was *learning* to believe them—or at least to fear that they might be true.

Martin took the days to further his own desires, to study the Kanans closely. He could have called it part of his duty as Alien Contact Officer, but he knew it wasn't, because he learned their customs and mores as he had learned no others on the many worlds he had seen.

Everything was sharing and joy on Kana. Even the work was made easy by singing and games. Morning and night, as the sun rose and fell, the people gathered to face the light, and Chantuka offered prayers to their God. "Greeting the sun," it had been called by Martin's own people; thanking God for the light and life He gave them each day. The serenity on the Kanans' faces reached inside Martin and twisted into a ball, fighting something else that crouched there.

One thing he knew. These people were different. Most of the aliens he had met were counterparts of Earthborn man. They waged their fights for survival on worlds varying in harshness and developed suitable degrees of ruthlessness to exist. They had benefited from contact and found good places in the galaxy.

But the Kanans had not fought their world. They had adapted to it. And Martin had an awful premonition that they would be trampled in the maze of machines and foreign humanity. It was like putting a fawn with a tiger, in the belief that the fawn would benefit.

Yet, in spite of the dread, he had to help win the treaty. The weaponless Kanans would be annihilated in an invasion.

When there were only two days left before the *Wasp* had to return to the *Astra,* Chantuka's wife was conspicuously absent from her place at the dawn ceremony. There was a frown under the dignity of the chief's face, and when he lowered his arms from the final gesture of the prayer, he turned immediately for his lodge and disappeared inside.

For once, Brandon had been observing the ceremony with Martin, and as Chantuka entered his lodge, Brandon followed him to investigate the woman's absence and the strange, new hush that hung over the village. Martin returned to the *Wasp* alone. Although Chantuka had become his friend, he didn't share Brandon's lack of consideration for the chief's privacy and didn't want to intrude on him.

When Brandon finally climbed up the ladder and into the *Wasp* a few minutes later, his face was red with haste and excitement. He kept his voice low as though he were discussing a secret, and since Martin was the only available crewman to talk to, he talked to him. "It's the chief's wife, all right. She's down—but good. Chantuka says she's been in pain all night."

"What's wrong with her?" Martin asked, worried. He liked the old woman, although he had seen little of her. She was just a quiet shadow in his mind, but a gentle, smiling shadow that hovered near Chantuka or her daughter, Tiva, or her son. "We haven't seen any disease all the time we've been here." Hayden, their biologist and medic, hadn't even been able to isolate anything on Kana that looked vaguely deadly.

Brandon frowned and stared him straight in the eye. "I don't like telling you this, and I want you to hold yourself in close check, Sunbear. You were deliberately left out of this decision. Now that it's all worked out, I suppose it's time for you to know. I said I needed something dramatic to work with, and I found it. What's wrong with her is our fault."

Martin stared back sharply.

"The old woman came out to the *Wasp* about twelve days ago on Hayden's invitation," Brandon said. "He showed her around his lab. Like we guessed, she lived up to the habits of all these backward savages and grabbed up one of the culture bottles because she thought it was pretty with the colored stuff inside it. It broke and cut her hand. She picked up the germ—or whatever. I'm no medic."

"Which culture bottle was it?" Martin's voice was reluctant because he was afraid of any answer.

Brandon's gaze was firm, meaning more than his words. "The one from the spikey plant we took two planets back. The one that killed that young botanist—Mason."

Martin was silent. He remembered the culture and the drab, lifeless planet which had produced it. Twelve days was the incubation period. It had taken twelve days for Mason to come down with it, and then Bowles had followed him, repeating the symptoms one day behind. Both botanists, they had both handled the spikey plant that transmitted the disease through innocent pricks. Mason had died. Bowles—.

Martin looked up, realizing why Brandon had given him that special stare.

"That's right," Brandon said. "You and Hayden saved Bowles, Sunbear. It was trial and error all the way, but you two saved him. You know the right antidote."

"Of course!" Martin surged to his feet, starting immediately for the lab and the antibiotic they had used for Bowles. If he was in time, he could save Chantuka's wife. She was old and her resistance must be lower than Bowles', but if he hurried—.

"Just a minute," Brandon called him to a halt.

"I don't have a minute!"

"I said, 'just a minute!'" Brandon assumed a tone that underlined his authority.

Martin came back.

"I've got orders for you, Sunbear. And they're full, command orders. You're not to tell Chantuka one word of this—understand? He isn't to know that we had anything to do with the disease. And when we save the woman, I want it stipulated that the treaty is the price. You're to help drive the point home."

"No." Martin said it flatly, cutting in on the end of Brandon's words. "You can't blackmail Chantuka with his wife's life."

"I have to." Brandon was dead sober.

"Not with *my* help. You shouldn't have told me you plotted this, Brandon. I won't go along with it. Not one filthy step. What would have happened if the bottle hadn't broken? Would you have injected her with it?"

"My motives are my business and go with my rank."

"But we should have started her treatment immediately! You knew that."

"She had to get good and sick for our plan to work. You and Hayden can start it now—with the treaty the condition for her cure."

"I will not agree to it," Martin spaced the words out and bit them off. "I won't abuse Chantuka this way. It's dirty. Did Evers know about it?"

"He did."

"And *he* went along with it?" Martin couldn't believe it of the missionary.

"He went along all the way. Why not, Sunbear? We've got the cure for her. A few days of being sick isn't too much to ask to seal the treaty. You just get underway and follow my orders."

Martin didn't move. Not one step.

"You're refusing my command?" Brandon demanded, his voice low.

"I am. Shoot me down where I stand—and right now—or I'll go and follow any course I think is decent enough, after what you've done." He stood still, waiting for Brandon's move, expecting a weapon to come out and put an end to the whole nasty affair.

Brandon let Martin's words register, then sighed, his face resigned to his frustration. "I don't execute my men. I'll leave that to your court martial. But be careful what you do because every action you take from this moment on goes into your record for prosecution. It's your choice." Suddenly his cold anger turned hot, and he cursed, "Dammit! What's so terrible about this? If we don't have the treaty, she'll die anyway! A lot of them will. When they're *forced* to come into line!"

Martin lifted the decorated material that served as a door, and stepped into the dim light of Chantuka's lodge. The chief was sitting on the sweet smelling, grass strewn floor by a low bed where his wife lay, gasping with her as she struggled for shallow, quick breaths. He was holding her hand in his own, engulfing it in a gesture of compassion and aching love.

The chief's son stood quietly in one corner, shadow-lit by the small fire that raised weak yellow flames in the center of the lodge. Tiva knelt by the fire, stirring some spicy brew in a large earth-colored pot. She looked at Martin once, then lowered her eyes, and her efforts at stirring told him more than her eyes had said. She was defeated and ready to grieve.

He had seen the same body expression in the people waiting outside, circling the lodge silently, caught in a still moment of time between faint life and creeping death.

Martin crossed to Chantuka and knelt beside him. He placed one hand on the old man's shoulder, then stared down at the woman. She was newly frail, her bronze skin glistening with the sweat of the disease, her eyes shut, her mouth slightly open to grasp in air.

Martin shuddered. He knew she was in pain because Mason and Bowles had both cried out in their pain; but she was making no sound.

He turned away from the sight of her and focused on Chantuka. He began feebly, "I—I—. You know that I'm sorry—."

"You have no need to say it," Chantuka told him. The hand he cradled in his own was thin and weathered with sun and work, and he clung to it as though it was the source of his life. He spoke to Martin softly, his voice deep but never trembling. "I cannot understand this. It is something I have never seen. She has been suffering." He placed both of his hands about the woman's small one and pressed it gently, gathered a great breath for himself, and said, "Death will come soon, and then the suffering will end for her."

Martin's mind leapt to what he felt was a ridiculous thought in view of what he knew, but he voiced it anyway. "Has your medicine man tried everything he knows to heal her?"

Chantuka met his eyes. "No. That cannot be done. I could not allow him to try."

"But why?" Martin had to struggle to keep his voice low. If the medicine man could possibly succeed there would be no need for the blackmailed treaty.

"Mr. Evers has told me many times of the anger of your God and I have to admit that I fear it. He forbids me to call our medicine man."

"Forbids!"

"I understand the reasoning of it. As Mr. Evers said, once we have heard of the true God, then we are bound to follow His ways or accept His punishment. I—. I cannot endanger my people with a plague from this place, 'Heaven.' I cannot allow them to suffer because I am weak and do what Mr. Evers calls 'backslide.' Perhaps I am a coward, but I have thought about this for all these days of her sickness."

At that moment Martin wanted nothing more than to spit on Evers for putting terror into a heart which had never held any. He knelt beside the old man, himself as confused as Chantuka. In his own heart he felt strongly the sense of purity the medicine man would bring, yet he couldn't believe with certainty, he couldn't risk a life on his own heart's emotion. Hayden had a needle full of liquid that *was* certain, and even though it meant the sealing of a terrible treaty, it also meant the saving of Chantuka's wife. And the chief needed that saving more than Martin Sunbear needed a demonstration of ancient religious purity.

"There is no other way for me than just to accept her death," Chantuka said. He was now strangely defiant, decision strengthening each line of his body. "She has had a long and happy life. She told me herself that she is content. Now, she sleeps. She will never wake."

Martin's eyes flashed with tears of pity and frustration and he stood up quickly, ready to tell Chantuka the truth about this disease and about Evers' Standardized God, but before he could speak a word, the lodge door lifted and Brandon strode in, followed by Hayden. The medic carried a medical kit.

Brandon started talking as soon as he was through the door. "I came back as soon as I could, Chantuka. Is she any better?"

Martin hated him for that question, but held his tongue.

Chantuka glanced up quickly at the intrusion, but only shook his head and whispered, "No. She cannot be."

"But she *can*," Brandon said. "Hasn't Sunbear told you about our plan for her? Our medicine?"

"I didn't have a chance," Martin told him, but Brandon's quick little sneer spoke paragraphs of snide understanding.

Brandon shoved his way in beside Chantuka. "Then I can be the one to give you the news, chief. There's a possibility that we can save your wife. Cure her. My crew and I." Brandon talked fast then, in his own simple grasp of the Kanan language, forcing Chantuka to understand that Hayden might be able to cure her with the wonderful power of Earth's medicines.

His explanation brightened Chantuka with its offer of hope, and the wrinkled face was suddenly eager. Chantuka rose to his feet to meet the captain eye to eye, searching Brandon's face as though he could read his sincerity right through his eyes.

Then Chantuka asked, "Martin Sunbear—is this all true? Should I let my heart be hopeful again?"

"It's true," Martin answered. "I was just ready to tell you when Captain Brandon came in."

"But I'm here now and I can handle it all," Brandon cut him short. "You just do the translating for me. This next part is essential." He swiveled suddenly to Hayden, "Call Mr. Evers. His Kanan is better than mine and he can check and see that Sunbear gets every word of what I say translated correctly."

Hayden moved quickly outside and Martin looked away, half turning his back, ashamed of what he knew he would have to speak in translation, and more ashamed of the fact that Brandon viewed him with such distrust that he had called for a watchdog.

Evers came in with Hayden and they all stood together in a tight little knot. Brandon cleared his throat meaningfully, spoke, and Martin swallowed his conscience and repeated the words, trying not to let them be a part of himself, trying to imagine himself as no more than the computer which could translate as well as he.

Brandon explained that he expected Chantuka's acceptance of their treaty if they did their best to restore his wife to him. Brandon didn't say, "If we *cure* her," but, "If we *try*," crafty even in the wording of his betrayal. Martin translated those words, too.

The Captain finished with a short, boasting pep talk about how the cure would prove to Kana once and for all time the worth of the things the galaxy had to give; their greatness and goodness.

As Martin finished his translation, something replaced the eagerness in the chief's attitude. Martin sensed it as desperate indecision and fear. By means of a single handclasp, Chantuka could save the life he valued most in the world; yet there was fear in him.

"Why are you holding back?" Brandon urged. "It's a simple and straightforward demonstration."

"I do not know," Chantuka spoke to Brandon, but gazed at Martin. "I feel that perhaps the two things cannot be weighed against each other—one life for a new and different future. I have a sense of foreboding."

They waited. The decision would be wholly Chantuka's. Whatever it was, Martin knew the woman would receive the treatment. Brandon couldn't keep him from that. He would inject the drug, himself.

He prayed silently that the Chief would refuse the bribe, then negated the prayer. The odds *had* to fall in Brandon's favor because there would be no future for the Kanans if they didn't.

Chantuka slowly paced the lodge, stopping once before Tiva and once before his son. Their feelings were clear. They wanted the life—their mother. He came back to Brandon and thrust his hand forward. "Perhaps it is because I am old that I hesitate. I am alone in my fear. I agree to let you try. Your people may come if your gifts prove good for us."

Martin grabbed up the medical kit and set to work before Hayden could even move to use his more professional knowledge. He motioned to the pile of blankets Evers had brought. "Warm those," he told Tiva. "Use stones—anything—but make them warm."

As the girl hurried to obey, he dug through the kit for the antibiotic that had saved Bowles' life. He thrust everything out of his mind but the urgent need to battle a disease. The rest would have to come later.

With the injection administered, he wrapped the frail old woman in the warm blankets Tiva supplied, then gave over at Hayden's insistence that he, as medic, should be in charge. Martin waited an hour in the far corner of the lodge with Chantuka's son, then went out into the center of the village.

The people were still there, still silent, and Martin picked out the medicine man, Ro-gon, among them. He was sitting with the rest, but with a difference about him. He wasn't simply waiting; he was agitated, his hands moving in twitches, his body struggling to sit there patiently when he hadn't been allowed to offer what he knew he had to offer. Martin veered away from Ro-gon.

He roamed the edge of the waiting people, paced up a way into the hills and came down again to reenter the lodge and check on the woman's response to the antibiotic. But there was no response; not the first time, nor the third. She lay just as before. Dying.

The hours dragged on with her gasps for breath, and they, in turn, grew weaker. She wasn't responding, and Hayden frantically tried new dosages, finally new methods, caught up, himself, in saving this life, treaty or no treaty. Chantuka remained near her, never letting his hope diminish, but Martin's hope plummeted. Something was wrong.

They had waited too long to start the treatment in the first place, callously letting her go too deeply into the clutch of the disease, ignoring the fact that she was old while Bowles had been young, that she had few antibodies of her own to defend her because she had lived her life on a planet that was disease free. Martin had known when he gave the first injection that it had to start its work in a matter of a few hours or it would never control the bacterial invasion, and those few hours were running out.

Finally, he went to the *Wasp,* his feet shuffling in the Kanan grass. Brandon was waiting in the ship's tiny lounge. "Any change yet?" Brandon asked.

Martin shook his head.

"It's getting pretty late in the game, isn't it?" Brandon sighed. "Well —we made the deal on the basis of our *trying,* not our curing. We still have the treaty, either way."

"Good for us," Martin muttered, and went to his own quarters.

It was dawn when Hayden returned, Evers behind him. They all met in the lounge. Hayden was exhausted, every line of his face deepened by the long day and night of working and watching. His first words were, "She's going to die. I can't stop it."

"You've given up?" Brandon demanded.

"I can't do anything else for her!" Hayden half shouted.

"I think we waited too long to begin," Evers put in.

"Is that the reason?" Brandon badgered Hayden.

"I don't know." Hayden slumped into a chair. "It could be. It's more likely the simple fact that she doesn't respond to our drugs in the same way we do. She's a different race. She's an alien. And she's dying. I came back to the ship because I didn't want to see the rest of it."

"And you?" Martin turned on Evers. "Didn't you stay to say your last words over her for Chantuka's benefit?"

Evers lashed back with the little strength he had left to muster, "I prayed for her all the time I stood in that litter strewn shack."

"I thought you did," Martin spat. "But your god of vengeance decided to *take* some this time, right?"

Evers looked at him in confusion.

"Listen, Sunbear–," Brandon started.

"*You* listen," Martin cut him short. "You admit you've failed, right, Hayden? And you admit *you've* failed, right, Evers?"

They both stared at him blankly.

"I'm taking your silence for 'yes.' So now I'm free to try the only way that's left."

"What does that mean?" Brandon stood up, expanding his chest with his authority.

"Don't worry, I won't endanger your treaty. Just stay out of my way. I'm taking *my* right to a chance. I want that woman to live! I may fail, myself, but if I do, I damn well won't run away from her last gasps. I'll stay by Chantuka and give him whatever support I can!"

He left the lounge at a run and half slid down the ladder, heading full speed for the village and the thing he now saw clearly that he had to do.

He strode through the gathered Kanan people, only noting the exhausted, hopeless postures that had come upon them during the long night. It had become a death watch now and they were only sitting together to wait for it to fall.

He lifted the cover on Chantuka's lodge and stepped inside, halting his furious pace as the odor of sweat and pain and despair filled his senses. The lodge was dim. Tiva had let the fire burn itself down as her mother's life was burning down, and Chantuka's son had ceased his standing vigil to crouch in the corner, alone.

Chantuka turned from his place beside the bed and the old man's eyes were red and damp. "Thank you for coming, Martin Sunbear," he murmured. "But it still might be a long while. This death is slow."

Martin clasped the chief's shoulder, but with more urgency than sympathy. "We're not just going to wait for it, Chantuka. I've come to talk, and to find a way to help her."

"That is beyond us. Even your great medicine could not do it. Your Hayden poured out his heart in trying."

Martin clenched his teeth to force himself to speak the next words softly, "Our Hayden *caused* it, Chantuka. Our Hayden and our Brandon and our Evers."

The old man's tired mind couldn't comprehend, and Martin began to explain, slowly, in the best Kanan he could find, how the plot had been laid to infect the chief's wife, to let her sicken to the crisis point, and then bargain for the treaty with her life.

Chantuka showed one tall moment of shocked anger, his eyes glinting with fury. Then he said confidently, "You were not a part of this, Martin Sunbear."

"I was not. But I heard of it and I didn't tell you. I heard of it yesterday. After that, my only thought was to save her. I am ashamed. We've always had the truth between us."

"No." Chantuka rose from his place and strode to stand near the ebbing fire. "It is a dishonorable treaty, but *you* are not dishonored. I think I understand. It cannot matter now—anymore. I have made the treaty and *my* honor is good even though your fellowmen have none. I have lost, have I not. I was not wise enough to see into them."

"You haven't lost your wife yet, Chantuka. There is still hope for her. Use your *own way*. Call your medicine man."

Chantuka shrank away, ashamed to admit his fear. "Mr. Evers said that—."

"Forget what Evers said! His god is not yours. Call on your own god, Chantuka. Evers has no place in your mind at all. He *agreed* to this betrayal. He cannot be the holy man you thought he was."

The chief turned Martin's words in his mind, reluctant to decide too hastily again. He finally said, "You speak the truth. He could not be what I thought, and so his vengeful god may not be true, either. My duty then is to my wife. She has been the victim. Perhaps I can save her, at least." He swung to his son, "Ask Ro-gon to come to us. We will try our own way."

When Ro-gon, the tribal medicine man came, Martin quickly learned what methods he would use to attempt the cure, and as he heard, he felt hope seep into him, hope that came from ancient prayers and powers he had studied and stored secretly, but steadfastly.

He made a quick examination of the old woman and judged that death was still many hours away. Mason had gone through this stage of the disease and hadn't died for another twelve hours after its onset. If Ro-gon failed in his attempt, then her death would inch itself out to the end. But there *was* time to try.

He desperately wanted to make a request of Chantuka. He doubted if he had the right, but in the dim lodge, with the fire glowing down to its own death, he said softly, "Chantuka—may I stay and stand with you? I'm not a member of your family—not even of your people—but I want to add my soul to your prayers. I want it so much."

Now Chantuka was the one to clasp Martin on the shoulder. "You are welcomed, and thanked. I am very tired, and your added strength will help to fill my place."

Ro-gon interrupted. "What is your people's way, Martin Sunbear? Can you adapt to ours?"

"The two ways are almost alike. I feel that I should purify myself, but there isn't time. Even so, while you prepare, I'll go to the stream and wash myself—get the dirt and feel of the *Wasp* off my body. I promise not to make you wait. I'll be back before you begin."

He went from the lodge and paced through the people. This time they were more alive in their faces. The sight of Ro-gon going to Chantuka had given them new hope. They would sit together and pray, now—silently, or perhaps aloud, in chants—but they knew they were at last free to help.

Martin washed himself quickly in the cold water, letting the chill cleanse more than his skin, and then the sun warm more than his body. He didn't dress again. He only put on his trousers.

He pulled from his pocket a thing that he had always kept hidden except at United Indian Nation meetings. It was a thin necklace of sinew, and hanging from it was a painted leather symbol of the Sun which was one representation of the Great Spirit. He put it on proudly, and looking around himself at the beauty of this world, let the sense of peace it brought wash him cleaner still.

Evers' angry voice broke his mood. "What have you done? I just saw that witch doctor in Chantuka's shack. You've led that man to backslide! After all my work! This can't be excused, Martin."

"Then, don't excuse it. Just get out of my way because I'm going to join them in that 'shack' and cure that betrayed old woman."

Evers' eyes fell on the painted symbol. "That! That thing–! You've lost your mind, Martin. What *is* that?"

"It's my cross, Mister Evers."

He started away, needing to hurry, but Evers was suddenly and wildly up against him, grabbing at his arms, wrenching at him to hold him back.

"I won't allow this, Martin!" Evers panted. "You've got to stop it right here!"

Martin grappled back, restraining himself from using all of his strength. He didn't want to hurt the slender missionary, but he had to break free. They tugged and pulled and then Martin thrust his full shoulder and weight into Evers, sending him backwards to sprawl on the ground, staring up, astonished.

"I'm sorry," Martin said. "But I'm following my own conscience. And I'm advising you and the rest of the crew to stay out of the village. The people won't be happy to see you right now."

The Kanans had positioned themselves in a perfect circle when Martin returned, and Chantuka's son and another man were edging slowly out of the lodge, carrying the bed with Chantuka's wife lying on it, eyes closed, her breast barely rising anymore as she had even stopped the hard gasping for breath. They placed the bed in the center of the circle, full in the sunlight, and the stranger took his place with the rest. Only Ro-gon, Chantuka's son, and Tiva remained on their feet. Chantuka was the last to appear from inside the lodge.

Martin went to the standing group hesitantly. He was out of place here and felt it, suddenly, but Chantuka took his arm and placed him in position facing the sun. Their shadows fell in long lines behind them, reaching like fingers into the crowd of silent Kanans.

Ro-gon approached him. The medicine man had not changed his clothing or put on any special symbols. He remained just as he had been, but there was something new in his posture—a confidence, a power—that emanated from him as he reached inside himself for the gift of understanding God had given to him. The power that allowed him to heal.

He spoke very softly to Martin. "You must release your spirit now, Martin Sunbear. Free yourself of your machines and potions and lift your mind to the True Source of help and love. As I look at you, I believe you can do this. I hope you succeed, because one false spirit could influence our work here. She is very old and very close to death."

"I understand," Martin answered him squarely. "And I know I can do it, Ro-gon, or I would never stand here with you. Your people are all of one mind now, and I'll join you in that. I am stripped down to my soul, and I think that soul is good."

"Your eyes say that it is," Chantuka murmured, and moved to stand closer to him.

For a moment, Martin wondered where he had found the simple words. There was something in the Kanan language, itself, something that described the world and its meanings in gentleness that allowed even an alienated man like himself to rise to the level of the true people around him.

He had little time to wonder at it because Ro-gon immediately walked to stand beside the old woman's bed. The Holy Man stared down at her for long, silent seconds, then raised his face to the sun, and all the faces in the circle around him lifted toward the sky.

It was time to begin.

Martin raised his own head, feeling the rays as heat, as tangible light on his cheeks and forehead, and his hand came up to clutch the symbol he wore against his chest.

Today he would make one sun out of two. Across the stars—one sun.

Ro-gon spoke to the sky and the wind. "We have brought Your daughter back into Your sunlight, Great Father, where she has lived and where You intend that she should always live. Take her back to Yourself again and let her open her eyes and breathe Your air gently as You commanded things to be many ages ago. She has suffered, but it was not of Your making. Your people gathered here know this. We ask now that You deliver her to us again, that her years may still be as You intended—loving, gentle, and good. We ask it with one voice—the voice of Your people.

"You placed Your hand on me in dreams and told me that I could speak these things for others. I am speaking them now. Great Father, Creator of all and Love of all, please hear us. Let Your daughter be well. Let the sun return into her life. We ask it, Great Father."

There was total silence over the village. Not even a bird called from the trees. Not an insect hummed in the grass. It was as if the world were waiting, staring to the sky, listening for an answer.

Martin waited, too, his hand tight on his painted symbol as he prayed "Great Spirit" and "God."

Then he closed his eyes because the sky was dazzling him with flecks of white and dancing motes. His mind tried to stray from the thought Ro-gon was expecting him to hold, and he heaved it back quickly. He knew this could take time. It might require hours of waiting and repeating. He would wait them out with the rest.

He couldn't tell time except by the feel of the sun slowly passing across his skin and the sky, but he judged it to be better than an hour before Ro-gon again cut the silence with his deep voice and called on the Great Father to imbue him with the gift He had bestowed on him in his dreams; to reach down for His daughter and let her know that life was still within her and her years were not yet spent.

"You ordained that she be happy, Great Father, and she was happy until this unknown thing fell upon her. And it is an unknown thing, since it is not of Your making. It cannot harm her or bring her to death since it is not of You. You do not harm. Your world and Your people are both gentle and good. Please whisper to her the truth once more so that she may open her eyes and draw safe breath. We all wait, Great Father, for Your choice. And this choice, of course, we will accept."

The silence came again.

But then it was broken by a soft murmuring from the gathered people. The murmur took form and grew into a quiet, repeated chanting. Over and over it sounded, in words that Martin didn't know. He listened and at last decided that they weren't really words at all, just round and quiet sounds. He should have known at once. These people would not repeat prayers aimlessly until they became nothing, meant nothing. The sounds, with their roundness and rhythm, were only manifestations of the spirits that were making them; praying, waiting. He quickly learned the pattern and joined the chant, hearing Chantuka take voice beside him.

"She sees!"

It was Ro-gon's voice that sliced the chant in two, and every head turned to look at Chantuka's wife.

It was true. The woman's eyes were open, gazing at the sky. She weakly turned her head to find Chantuka, but she didn't need to search long because he was beside her in three strides, kneeling down to touch her face with his own old hands.

"Breathe!" Ro-gon said.

Her expression was one of confusion and bewilderment, but she opened her lips and drew in a short, harsh breath; then raised her whole upper body in one great long sigh of life-giving air.

Chantuka cradled her face in his hands and leaned over her to lay his cheek against hers, hiding the tears that had started to course down his face.

And Martin breathed, too. All around him came a great sigh as the people breathed in and out with her. He hadn't realized he had been nearly holding his breath, but now the air hit his lungs clean and spicy with the touch of Kana.

Ro-gon stood where he had been and lifted his face to the sun again, smiling this time.

"Thank You, Great Father," he called, loudly, vibrantly. "Your people thank You for one more proof of Your great Love."

Martin felt tears on his own cheeks and suddenly wanted to get away from this place. The emotion was too much. The Power demonstrated here was too much.

He glanced at the old woman, noted that her color was beginning to return to her lips and fingers already, said a silent "Thank You" of his own, and walked out of the circle. He had no shadow as he walked now, because the sun was at its zenith. So he walked alone on the Kanan grass.

He had intended to wander and sort out his thoughts, but half a mile from the village he was met by an angry group, standing to watch him approach. He considered turning in the opposite direction, but decided against that. He could face them now. He had gained new power, himself.

Three men confronted him; Captain Brandon, Hayden, and an infuriated Mr. Evers. He wondered idly why Lyler never seemed to make himself part of anything that went on with the crew. But Lyler seldom had.

Brandon, as usual, was the first to open his mouth. "How come you've been free to fraternize down there, Sunbear, when you told Mr. Evers we should all stay out?"

"And how come you listened to me and *stayed* out?" Martin threw the question back without an answer.

"None of us are fools, Martin," Hayden said. "You're Alien Contact Officer so when you warn us about the natives, we believe you."

"I'm starting to think he's more *alien* than alien *contact,*" Brandon complained, eyeing Martin suspiciously. "So—what happened? Did the high mucky muck do his magic tricks and shake his rattles?"

Martin kept his tone quiet and level. "He saved Chantuka's wife."

Only Hayden, of the three of them, showed relief at the news. Brandon was confounded, his face red, his veins bulging.

Mr. Evers' whole skinny body was a fist of frustrated anger crying for a target. "That was probably the effect of Hayden's drugs—if it's true at all. The drugs undoubtedly just took effect."

"I don't think so," Martin answered. "But it doesn't matter. The point is, she's going to survive. Why aren't you happy about it, Mr. Evers? Can't you rejoice with the rest of her people?"

"*At what you did?* You—you—," Evers fought for expression, then it rushed out of him without any control. "Martin Sunbear, you led those people down the road to hell, do you know that? You took their hands out of mine, out of God's and the Standard Faith, without a thought to what you were doing to them. I *had* those people. They were ready. And now it will take so much to bring them back!"

"Back to what?" Martin asked, still quietly.

"To God, you foolish—you *fool!* They have to come. The treaty is made and colonies will be established and those savages have to fit in with us. They were ready!"

"Out of fear," Martin said.

"Out of an awakening in their souls of who God is and what He will do to them if they don't follow His commands. But you walked in there with that blasphemous painted—. You sent Chantuka back to his paganism—to pagan gods for a cure. You've made heathens out of them again. If I were a violent man—if I were given to physical force—."

"Go on and hit me, Evers. Just don't be surprised when I don't fall down. I've seen something today that I always knew existed but that I could never find. It was beautiful and it was true and it worked!"

"Paganism! Heathenism!"

"I don't care what you call it, Evers, but I saw God working. These people *have* God. Right here and now. A closer kinship with Him than you have. More understanding."

Evers scoffed, "Oh, come, Martin."

"Then how do you explain it? Hayden gave her all that our science can offer, but she was dying in spite of him. You prayed for that woman, Evers. You called on God's mercy for her, but she was dying in spite of *you.* One lone 'heathen' medicine man, uniting himself with God as he knows God, gave that woman back to her husband and children. I wasn't certain before that what I felt shoving me from the soul out was right, but now I *know!*"

Evers cut in, "You admitted you were raised in a rubbish pile of religion, Sunbear. Emotionalized Christianity plus your own redman's heathenism."

"Emotionalized Christianity? You're calling Christ's healings emotionalism, aren't you? Then, why did it work for her? I've read the old Bible, I've already admitted that. My parents gave it to me to read. And if you've read it, then you have to remember the passage where Jesus Christ said, *'He that believeth on me, the works that I do shall he do also.'* That includes healing, Evers. So I'm right according to what you call emotionalized Christianity.

"I'm also right according to the religion of my so-called redman ancestors. They healed, too, whether you like the idea or not. While they still had the Earth and their innocence and their faith, they could heal, too! I should have believed my own soul all along. I shouldn't have needed proof like I had this afternoon. But now I *know!*"

Evers met him anger for anger. "You're saying I'm a thing of the devil. That I'm evil and stupid and soulless."

"I'm saying nothing of the sort. Your intentions are only good, Evers, and I realize that. Your own heart is decent, but you're bent on destroying a perfect people and their pure relationship with God in spite of that—just because they happen to worship Him differently and call Him by a different name.

"One God is one God, Evers. And they already have Him. Just as my people had Him. I won't let you force them to lose Him and then spend the rest of eternity trying to struggle their way back Home!"

"The Kanans have no choice, Martin!" Evers was shocked at his harangue. "You can't stop the treaty from proceeding to its final end, and if the Kanans don't adapt to our colonials, they're going to be physically injured. Perhaps destroyed! So what you're demanding for them —this insulation—can only be brought about in one way. Are you going to ask them to follow that one way? To commit racial suicide as your brother Navajo's tried to do? Do you actually want their *blood* just because of a lack of roots you feel in yourself, Martin?"

Martin stood perfectly still, his mind and body rolling in a great surge of emotion. Evers had hit the sorest spot of all. He was falling to pieces right in front of the three of them and he had no place to hide. They could never understand what he meant.

He grasped the painted symbol again, drew a shivering breath, and said only, "Forget the 'Martin'. My name is Sun Bear. A true and old Dakota name."

He spun around and paced away, then ran, needing the haven of his favorite hillside near the village to still his mind and help him evaluate what had happened to him and whether or not Kana could possibly be saved.

The hill held the same serenity it had always held, but he couldn't respond to it. He was too hard pressed, attacked from too many sides by doubts and terrors about his own motives and about Kana's future.

Memories and stories pulled at him, taking him back through years he had never seen to days he only knew through books and legends told at UIN meetings. Why should they be so real? What had happened to him here on Kana? Something terrible had happened and he wanted to stamp it all down, strangle it, bury it, deny it completely. Those days weren't his to own, but they were twisting him apart.

He moved into the shade of an arching tree where birds whisked in and out of the heavy-leafed branches, piercing the day with pipings. He cast his eyes down onto the village. There was so much inside him that wanted to be part of that village, to live in a past he had believed dead—but he had no place there. No right there. He had helped save Chantuka's wife, but even that act had only required convincing the chief to call on Ro-gon. He had stood with them in the healing prayers, but it would have been done without him just as well.

So he still had no home.

And as he looked at it objectively, from this higher vantage point, his body pressed against the grass and a large winged butterfly making flirting passes at the blue color of his trousers, he stilled the aching the scene brought to him. Stilled it deliberately.

This was not a hillside on the plains of Earth. He did not wear feathers in his hair. He did not ride a painted horse. That was gone. Forever. Tatters of it appeared at the UIN meetings, but they were tatters and nothing more. So he had to accept the rest of his life as it came to him. He would have to remain an alien among his own kind; a homeless man, keeping his own counsel.

Grief broke over him and he shuddered with it.

The village below took on the look of a stage with a pantomime being played out for him. Pitifully, he already knew the climax.

The people were busy, streaming in and out of their lodges, slowly changing before him from their normal clothing to brighter colors—to decorations, to ornaments—and he understood, at last, that they were preparing for a celebration, a time of thanksgiving for the life that had been given back to them.

Thanksgiving!—while their fate was still sealed tight in Brandon's and Chantuka's handclasp. The treaty was made. Colonists would come and dig into Kana, sending their machines down into the ground to scoop out foundations for wooden houses that would eventually turn to plastic when it could be manufactured in new factories supplied by the ore the new miners produced.

Evers would also have his way. The Standard Faith would be taught—that hodgepodge that really meant nothing. The Kanans would have to adapt themselves in order to be absorbed and changed into images of the larger civilization. If they didn't, they would meet fear, hatred, prejudice, and be abused.

If he told Chantuka the truth about the future, then the old chief in his outraged honor would deny the treaty and be faced with an invasion he didn't even know could come.

There was no way out. Only destruction lay at the end of every course. And he, Martin Sunbear, hadn't helped at all.

He watched the village and allowed the sight to lull him into feeling part of it, enjoying the bright clothes, the ornaments, because it was the last time he would see it. When the *Wasp* left Kana, he would never come back again.

He was soothed by the hill and the birds and the village until the afternoon had almost worn away. Time slipped by him as he conjured drum beats to go with the rising smoke of cooking fires and composed songs to sing at the thanksgiving ceremonies.

Then some women came partway up the hill, gathering flowers and grasses for the celebration, and they woke him from his revery. As he watched them work and admired their necklaces of shells and tiny feathers, another stab slapped through him.

Among those natural decorations he caught sight of cheap jewelry from his own culture; plastic combs, glass necklaces of many colors glinting in the sunlight, wristwatches that were given out simply as pretty bracelets and had no working parts.

"Insidious!" he cried, and was on his feet before he realized it. The women looked up at him, but he turned his back.

He paced further up the hill, hating himself for the wasted time, for accepting defeat. He might not ever return to Kana, but the destruction would occur just the same. Here he stood in the position where no one had stood when his own ancestors needed help. He wouldn't turn his back. He had to find a way to stop the ruin. *There had to be a way!*

He would wrestle with his mind on this hill until he found it.

When he returned to the *Wasp* it was dusk, the day almost drained away, but his step was firm and quick, his strength full, because he had found a plan and the new Sun Bear could do anything necessary to preserve this adopted culture, withstand anything Brandon might throw at him, hold his own emotions close—anything—to win his argument and convince Brandon of the good in the one way he had found.

The *Wasp* sat with its nose in the air, spotlights making a bright circle around it as the night gathered. Martin climbed the ladder to the lock and went inside. He found Brandon alone in the radio room, grateful that he was alone. He had to have the captain to himself if there was going to be any chance for this at all.

Brandon was working on some papers and when he looked up his face was immediately hostile. "Where'd you go? Off to beat your tom-toms?"

"Off to think," Martin said, putting humility into his voice.

Brandon's hostility began to fade. "Good. And since you came back to the *Wasp,* I take it you've made the right decision. I'm glad, Sunbear. I hate to see a good officer go alien crazy. So—rejoin the crew and come to our party. We're breaking out everything we've got tonight. It's time to whoop, boy."

"You couldn't really want me after this afternoon," Martin played on with his humility. "Not after what I did."

To his surprise, Brandon showed a little tooth in a smile. "You got carried away. So what? I've seen it once or twice before. Alien crazy. You contact men sometimes go slightly mad. I can understand that. Carried away. Hell, I'm carried away, myself! I can barely wait out the hours until the *Astra*'s in position and I can get on that radio and tell them what we've done down here. This is *big,* Sunbear. The biggest planet find we've made. So untouched and all here for us. It's going to guarantee my future. Yours, too."

"I don't want any credit," Martin said evenly.

Brandon dropped his pencil and spread his hands on the papers he was preparing, clearly deciding to ignore the edge he had heard in Martin's voice. "Give yourself some time. You're no more a savage than I am."

When Martin made no reply, Brandon continued, actually trying to make excuses for him. "You've been edgy all through this contact, Sunbear. I've seen it. I'm not a captain for nothing, you know. And—I'm willing to forget it happened. This once. Agreed?"

Martin hesitated. This was the moment to make his beginning, but he didn't know how. He could only find one way; bluntly, and with the whole truth. "It's not agreed, captain. I'm sorry. I said I'd been thinking. The trouble is, I didn't come to the conclusions you think I did. I don't like the treaty. We shouldn't interfere with these people."

"Interfere?" Brandon snatched at the word, caught off balance by what he had believed to be a reconciliation and had now turned sour on him. "Since when has contact for mutual advancement been called interference?"

"It will change their entire way of life."

"Of course it will. It will lift them right up off their skins and flowers and put them in the space age." He eyed Martin closely. "This thing's still eating you up, isn't it? Well, tell me what's in your head, Sunbear. I really do want to know."

Now was his time to catch Brandon's mind or lose it. "The Kanans will never be able to stand against our civilization, captain. This isn't an ordinary culture. Not anything like the ones we usually find. We'll introduce things here that have never been here before—lust, greed —all of our sins and more. We have no right to contaminate it."

"That part of it's up to Evers and his kind. Don't be a fool, Sunbear. These people are ripe. And who are we to say 'no' when they want us?"

"They don't know what they're doing."

"We can't even talk anymore, can we? You've got steel inside your brain and it won't budge an inch. Give Chantuka some credit. We told him what we have to offer and he wants it. All we want to do is *give* it to him. To all of them. We'll give a thousand times more than we gain."

It was starting to go wrong, but Brandon's mind was still slightly open, so Martin sucked in his breath and went wholly on the offensive. "So far we've given them gambling, rape, and the near death of a beloved old woman."

"That wasn't my fault. How was I to know about the drug resistance? She didn't die. Even if she had, one death is better than genocide. And the future we'll give them will more than compensate for—."

Martin whirled on him, his voice hollow, "There are times when 'giving' is not appropriate, Brandon; when it's more 'taking away.' When it's a benevolent, but insidious destruction. If they really knew what's in your hands, maybe they wouldn't want what you've got."

Brandon's own voice was suddenly quiet and calm. "Now it's what *I've* got? You're dropping out of the picture again? Just when did this total alienation happen, Sunbear?"

"I don't know. Maybe two hundred years ago when my own people were given the 'great gifts' of an advanced civilization. When they discovered that they had to trade dignity and God for felt hats with feathers sticking in them!" He forced himself to hold in, and went closer to Brandon. "I want to save these people from that fate. I want to do for them what no one did for us. I'm asking you to help me."

Brandon was too dumbfounded, and too nervous because of his proximity, to give a sensible answer. "You *are* crazy. Just *plain* crazy!"

"Try to understand. Please. This is something I have to do and I can't help myself. I've cooperated with you all the way so far. Now I'm pleading with you to go along with *me*."

Brandon made a valiant attempt to make his voice soothing. "Look, Sunbear, I can't do anything. Without the treaty, there will be invasion for them. You don't want that, and there's no way around it."

"There *is* a way. The one thing that makes a planet off-limits to us forever. Quarantine! We can report that Kana isn't safe. We can quarantine Kana so no one else will ever come here. The other men will go along, I think. They've liked it here too much to want to hurt these people. I'm positive of Hayden. And Lyler and Evers can be persuaded."

"That's treason!" Brandon dropped his pretense and let the words roar out.

"But it will work, captain. Once a planet is quarantined, no one else ever comes to it. That's the law! And we can stay here. We're not important, anyway. The issue overshadows us."

Brandon shook his head. "Your plan defeats your own purpose. Having us around would be just as influential to the natives as having colonials around."

"We can risk that. At least there's a chance my way. Your way, there's nothing."

"No, Sunbear, it's out of the question. You're sick—not responsible—but you're wrong. You're a total misfit. *You* don't care if you ever go home or not. But, I do!" Brandon suddenly darted to the left and jammed his fingers on the red emergency button.

With the quick motion, Martin almost responded out of panic, almost attacked, but stopped himself short. The alarm sounded, screaming through the ship, and immediately the clank of answering feet pounded over their heads.

"There was no need for that," Martin said. "I'm not going to attack you, Brandon."

Hayden and Lyler appeared at the door, but Brandon motioned them to stay outside. "Now, Sunbear—do I lock you up for the rest of our stay? Or do you behave yourself?"

"No!—no lockup," Martin muttered. His mind was racing, trying to sort possibilities. All he knew was that he had to remain free. "I won't bother you anymore. You have all the cards, anyway. I can't hurt you. I know that and so do you."

Brandon looked hard at him, then shrugged. "For once, you're right.

Just be here when it's time to radio the *Astra.* I want some sign from you that you're still a member of this crew."

"You'll have it. I'll be beside you all the way." He left, brushing past Lyler and Hayden who were still tensed for trouble. They let him pass.

He arrowed straight for Chantuka's village. Reporting Kana unfit for habitation was still the only way out. Brandon had blocked it, but it was still the only way. And he was still the only one who was willing to do it.

As he came to the edge of the village, he decided one thing surely. He would tell Chantuka the truth about Kana's actual choice in the treaty. If nothing else, he had to relieve his conscience of the lies.

The old chief met him at the doorway of his lodge, but Martin brushed by him and entered gravely, only nodding hello to Tiva. Then, giving the chief no chance to speak, he rushed right into the tale of treachery he had to tell.

Chantuka listened with his eyes wide at first, then his face closed down, revealing nothing. But when Martin finished, Chantuka exploded in protest. "How could anyone do that? They would actually come in great numbers and kill us? No! How could anyone be so cruel?"

Martin looked at the grassy floor of the lodge. He couldn't explain this to Chantuka any more than he had really managed to explain the dead rabbit to Tiva.

Chantuka protested a moment more, and then stopped, accepting what he had heard whether he understood it or not. There was only sadness in him, all directed at Martin. "It was hard for you to go along with those things. And even harder for you to tell me about them. I thank you for your courage."

"It didn't do either of us any good," Martin answered.

"No. The wicked men have won this time. But I have made the treaty, so I must stand by it."

"And you would, because of honor and everything else you believe in," Martin said, and it was almost a curse. "It's still up to me to keep you from being destroyed."

"But you have already tried. Your captain said no to your plan."

"It was a true plan, even so. And it still is!" Martin met Chantuka's eyes for the first time since he had entered the lodge. "Chantuka—will you trust me enough to do as I ask?"

"I would have to be made of rock not to trust you now."

"Then—one question. If I do what I have in mind to do, the crewmen will be very angry. They might even try to harm you. How would you handle that?"

"We would defend ourselves as we always do against wicked men," Chantuka said. "We would have to send them to the Judgement Place."

Martin's skin grew cold. "And this place? Is—is it a place of dying, Chantuka? Would they be killed? I don't—."

"The Judgement Place is not for killing, Martin Sunbear. It is only a place apart. Do you understand? A place where the wicked ones go to be kept away from the people. They are not harmed. Not even physically restrained."

Now it was Martin's turn not to understand.

Tiva spoke up, "It is the place for the ones who are not willing, for the ones who do evil things." She laughed, looking to her father, "Martin Sunbear thinks we are all good on Kana, father. I know that from my talks with him."

"All good?" Chantuka smiled a little. "That would be impossible. Sometimes we find a wicked one, and then he must go to the Judgement Place. There he is in the hands of God. He has all he needs in food and shelter. Unfortunately, he even has companionship since there are others who have been sent there before him. But he is not allowed to come back among us."

"We keep a watch, even so," Tiva finished the explanation. "To be sure all is well with them."

"Of course! Ostracism! I should have guessed. My own ancestors practiced ostracism." Martin sighed, relieved. "That leaves my way clear, then. I can follow my plan. Again, Chantuka—will you trust me?"

"There is no need for you to ask. Yes, I will trust you."

"Then, listen carefully. We haven't much time. I'm going back to the *Wasp* and a few minutes after I leave, I want you to come to the ship with every man in the village. I want you to make a loud noise about it. Act angry, threatening—anything you can think of that will draw the crew out of the *Wasp*."

"But why?" Chantuka asked simply.

"To give me time alone inside. There is only one way to save your world, and I'm going to take it."

"Then—we shall help you. Trust *us*, now."

With Chantuka's words, he left, running the distance to the *Wasp*. It was quiet inside the ship and he didn't go to Brandon. Let the captain think he was still gone. When the time came, Brandon would know he was there in capital letters. He went into his own cabin, leaving the door ajar so he could hear. It wasn't many minutes before a low, buzzing sound came from outside the *Wasp,* and grew until it was discernible as the shouts of men.

Brandon's voice echoed in the metal corridor, "Somebody find out what the devil's going on out there!"

Footsteps hammered to the lock and Hayden shouted, "It's the whole village coming, captain. They've got clubs in their hands."

"Where's Sunbear?" Brandon hollered. "Sunbear!"

"I'm here." Martin strode into the corridor. Everyone was by the outer lock, watching the mob of Kanans who were coming, waving their clubs and shouting angry Kanan words.

"What do you make of this?" Brandon demanded.

"I can't make anything of it. They've never been hostile, you know that."

"Then they're probably not hostile now? Is that what you're saying?"

"They look it, but I doubt if they intend anything," Martin hedged.

"Our first duty is to protect the ship," Brandon decided. "We'll just get out there and—."

"You wouldn't use weapons on them!" Martin gasped. His plan couldn't backfire against Chantuka now.

Brandon hesitated—then, "No—no I suppose not. We'll try to talk first, but if it turns out to be necessary, you're going to lose some of your blessed 'brothers.' " Brandon's eyes were mean. "Everybody outside. Act friendly, but stand firm."

Martin hung back while the four men exited the ship. As Lyler's foot left the ladder and touched ground, Martin shut the door and locked it. The crew of the *Wasp* was outside—locked out by sheer, bare metal —and he was alone to do what had to be done. He laughed to himself as he went to the radio room. Chantuka had managed to look more menacing than he had thought possible.

Sudden pounding on the outside of the ship didn't stop him. Brandon wanted back inside. But Brandon wouldn't get back inside. Not until the *Astra* had been contacted and the false report given. He sat down at the radio, warmed the apparatus for sending, and waited out the final minutes before contact time. The pounding on the hull continued for a while and then stopped. But he was certain the men were safe in Chantuka's hands, so he paid no attention. They would live, every one of them—simply cut off from all fraternization.

The minutes went by and contact time ticked up. He opened the switches and called into the radio, "*Astra—Astra*—this is the *Wasp*."

"Brandon?" a tinny voice asked after a long minute's wait. "This is the *Astra*. Is that you, Brandon?"

Martin braced himself for the final lie. "This is Martin Sunbear of the *Wasp*. Brandon is dead. They're all dead! I'm the only one left alive. Repeat—the crew is dead. This planet harbors a plague. Quarantine!" His voice shook with the lie and the knowledge that he was condemning Brandon, Lyler, Hayden and Evers to spending their lives here, to never seeing home again. But he wanted the tremors in his voice. They gave credence to his next words. "The fever's rising in me now. This is the only report I'll be able to make. This planet is death. Men cannot survive here. Repeat—*cannot survive!*"

"Sunbear!" the tinny voice cried. "For God's sake—everyone else is dead?"

"Everyone."

"Is there anything we can do for you, man? Any way we can get you off in time to—."

"Nothing," Martin gasped into the radio. "We tried everything in the medical book. There's nothing to be done—except to keep other men away from here. We couldn't even find the cause—not even the cause. Just place the quarantine and—."

"Of course. But, you! What about you?"

"I'm dead, *Astra*. Just place the quarantine. I'm signing off. I won't be calling again."

He switched off immediately, haunted by the compassion in the tinny voice from the *Astra*. He set about destroying the radio systematically, making sure there would never be a way to repair it. Then he destroyed the spare parts—and he was finished. The lie had gone out and no one would ever come to Kana again. No one. And no one would ever leave Kana, for without the radio, they couldn't home in on the *Astra*.

He waited in the corridor, catching his breath, feeling like a traitor and a savior at the same time. Brandon and the crew had to be faced and told. He would take their abuse and deserve it. But he had saved his half-home. And he could live out his life at least partially content, millions of miles from the Earth that had never fostered contentment in him.

He opened the outer lock and stepped into the spotlighted night, meeting the native faces that stared up at him blankly, searching out Chantuka. The old chief stood at the foot of the ladder and Martin went halfway down to talk to him.

"It's done," Martin told him. "I've arranged it so that you'll never be bothered by us again. That is a promise." He glanced about, ready to hear Brandon's curses, but Brandon and the other men weren't in the crowd. "Where is the captain?" he asked.

"I sent your fellow-men to the Judgement Place," Chantuka said, his face more lined than Martin had ever seen it.

"Already?"

"It was best not to wait and let them grow angry enough to injure someone—or themselves. I was sorry to do it, but we agreed, you and I, and I explained it to my people and they accepted it, too."

Martin sighed deeply, now having to say a thing he didn't want to say, but determined to follow his course honestly and honorably. "Then —I must join them."

He felt oppressed by the night. The sweet future he had won for these people was smothering him. He hung onto the railing, decision sure and final in him, but tearing at him in spite of the rightness of it. "I'll go now, if you'll have someone show me the way."

"No!" Chantuka cut in quickly. "That is not for you. You are not unwilling or wicked. You belong free with us."

Martin's heartbeat quickened with a sudden yearning, but he wouldn't allow it to influence him. "And now it's my turn to say 'no.' You have to understand one thing, Chantuka, and understand it well. Keep to yourselves—entirely. That even means to keep away from *me!* Don't ever give up anything you have to anyone. If you change with the years, let it be your *own* change. If you are ever visited again by some other alien race, don't offer that first ear of corn."

"Corn?" the wrinkled face was puzzled.

"Don't offer anything; and don't accept anything. The greatest gift any other civilization has to offer you is Nothing. You cannot benefit through them. You can only be hurt."

Chantuka nodded his white-haired head, understanding. "But what of you, Martin Sunbear? The man who saved us must stay with us. You need not go off with your comrades. I have seen it in your eyes that this is truly your home. It is strange, but I think perhaps you are one of us—inside. You could not, and *would* not hurt us."

Martin Sunbear clutched the railing hard. This choice was an unbearable one. Every pore of him cried out to accept Chantuka's welcome, but he didn't know if he should. He wanted it more than he had wanted anything in his life.

He raised his eyes to the dark sky and watched the wings of a night-bird beat the soft air near the spotlights, and as the bird called, high and pure, he let the truth come out of himself, confident that he was following the right path.

He said, as he looked back to meet Chantuka's eyes, "I believe it, too. In fact, I *know* it. I *can* live with you by watching myself closely so that I never influence you. I vow this—here where I stand. The first time I see myself influencing you, I will go and stay where Captain Brandon is. Forever."

Chantuka reached up and took his hand from the railing, pressing it firmly, sealing the vow. "That day will never come. And you will be a great man among us and become a legend. You will never be forgotten in our history. If strangers come, they will not be welcomed innocently again. We will be hard and isolate them before they can strike us. They will offer gifts, but the memory of my people is long, and they will always be compared to the man who saved us. The man-who-offers-gifts will never stand above the man-who-offered-nothing."

Martin Sunbear humbly stepped down into the crowd of Kanans to become one of them. His conscience about Brandon and the others would ease, and he'd personally see to it that they were all right. There was nothing to hurt them on this world, anyway.

As he walked tall and straight with his new people, he thought that it was strange to find that even a span of two hundred years had not been able to quiet the pound of blood and tradition that raced through his veins. He was stripped of all acquired civilization now. He could throw it off gratefully, knowing that when a man is so much alone, he goes back to what is true inside him.

Perhaps no one would ever understand why he had done it. They didn't matter.

Perhaps the god of the galaxy would not understand. But that didn't matter.

The God of Sun Bear would know—the Great Spirit, the kind and mighty God of the old times; the God Who lived with Kana.

The few who knew about the brotherhood of life would understand; and the soul of Tiva's little rabbit; and the spirits which had once belonged to bones that lay in ancient Earth, strewn with the remnants of eagle feathers.

forever and amen

By ROBERT BLOCH

FOREVER.

It's a nice way to live, if you can afford it.

And Seward Skinner could.

"One billion integral units," said Dr. Togol. "Maybe more."

Seward Skinner didn't even blink when he heard the estimate. Blinking, like every other bodily movement, involves painful effort when one is in a terminal stage. But Skinner summoned the strength to speak, even though his voice was no more than a husky whisper.

"Go ahead with the plan. But hurry."

The plan had been ten years in the making and Skinner had been dying for the past two, so Dr. Togol hurried. Haste makes waste and in the end it probably cost Skinner closer to five billion IGUS than the price quoted. Nobody knew for sure. All they knew was that Seward Skinner was the one man in the entire galaxy—the known galaxy, that is—who could afford the expenditure.

That was the extent of their knowledge.

Seward Skinner had been the wealthiest man alive for a long, long time. There were still a few oldtimers around who could remember the days when he was a public figure and a private joke—the Playboy of the Planets, as they called him. According to the rumors he had a woman on every world.

Other people, a trifle less elderly, recalled a more mature Seward Skinner—the Galactic Genius, fabulous inventor—entrepreneur of Interspace Industries, the largest corporate combine ever known. During those days his business operations made the news, and the rumors.

But for the majority of the interplanetary public, the youngsters without personal memories of those faroff times, Seward Skinner was merely a name. In recent years he'd withdrawn completely from any contact with the outside worlds. And Interspace Industries had carefully and painstakingly tracked down and acquired every tape, every record of his past. Some said these had been destroyed, some said the data had been hidden away, but in the end it amounted to the same thing. Seward Skinner's privacy was protected, complete. And nobody saw the man himself any more. His business, his life itself, seemed to be run by remote control.

Actually, of course, it was run by Dr. Togol.

If Skinner was the richest man, Dr. Togol was surely the most brilliant scientist. Inevitably, the two men were drawn together by a common love—wealth.

What wealth represented to Skinner no one knew. What it meant to Dr. Togol was plainly apparent; it was the tool of research. Unlimited funds were the key to unlimited experimentation. And so a partnership came into being.

During the past decade Dr. Togol developed his plan and Seward Skinner developed incurable cancer.

Now the plan was ready to function, just as Skinner was ceasing to function.

So Skinner died.

And lived again.

It's great to be alive, particularly after you've been dead. Somehow the sun seems warmer, the world looks brighter, the birds sing more sweetly. Even though here on Eden the sun was artificial, the light was supplied by beaming devices, and the birdsong issued from mechanical throats.

But Skinner himself was alive.

He sat on the terrace of his big house on the hill and looked down over Eden and he was pleased at what he had wrought. The bleak little satellite of a barren and neglected world he'd purchased many years ago had been transformed into a miniature earth, a reminder of his original home. Below him was a city very similar to the one where he'd been born; here on the hilltop was a mansion duplicating the finest dwelling he'd ever owned. Yonder was Dr. Togol's laboratory complex, and deep in the vaults beneath it—

Skinner shut away the thought.

"Bring me a drink," he said.

Skinner, the waiter, nodded and went into the house and told Skinner, the butler, to mix the drink.

Nobody drank alcohol any more, and nobody had waiters or butlers, but that's the way Skinner wanted things; he remembered how he'd lived in the old days and he intended to live that way now. Now and forever.

So after Skinner had his drink he had Skinner, the chauffeur, drive him down into the city. He peered out of the minimobile, enjoying the spectacle. Skinner had always been a people watcher, and the activities of these people were of special and particular interest to him now.

Behind the wheels of other minimobiles, the Skinners nodded and smiled at him as he passed. At the intersection, Skinner, the security officer, waved him along. On the walks before the fabrication and food processing plants, other Skinners went about their errands. Skinner, the hydroponics engineer, Skinner, the waste-recycler, Skinner, the oxygenerator control man, Skinner, the transport dispatcher, Skinner, the media channeler. Each had his place and his function in this miniature world, keeping it running smoothly and efficiently, according to plan and program.

"One thing is definite," Skinner had told Dr. Togol. "There'll be no computerization. I don't want my people controlled by a machine. They're not robots—each and every one of them is a human being, and they're going to live like human beings. Full responsibility and full security, that's the secret of a full life. After all, they're just as important to the scheme of things as I am, and I want them to be happy. It may not matter to you, but you've got to remember that they're my family."

"More than your family," Dr. Togol said. "They are you."

And it was true. They were him—or part of him. Each and every one was actually Skinner, the product of a single cell, reproduced and evolved by the perfection of Dr. Togol's process.

The process was called cloning and it was very involved. Even the clone theory itself was involved and Skinner had never completely understood it. But then he didn't need to understand; that was Dr. Togol's task, to understand the theory and devise ways to bring it to reality. Skinner provided the financing, the laboratory, the equipment, the facilities. His means and Dr. Togol's ways. And in the end—when the end came—his body provided the living cell tissue out of which the clones were extracted, isolated, and bred. The clones, cycling through complicated growth into physical duplicates of Skinner himself. Not reproductions, not imitations, not copies, but truly *himself*.

Glancing ahead towards the rearview mirror of the minimobile, Skinner saw the chauffeur, a mirror image of his own face and body. Gazing out of the window he saw himself again reflected in every form that passed. Each of the Skinners was a tall man, well past middle years, but with the youthful vigor born of a careful and painstaking regimen of advanced vitamin therapy and organ regeneration; the result of expensive medical attention that partially obliterated the ravages of metastasis. And, since the carcinoma was not hereditary, it had not been carried over into the clones. Like himself, all the Skinners were in good health. And, like himself, they carried within them the seeds—the actual cells—of immortality.

Forever.

They would live forever, as he did.

And they were him. Physically interchangeable, except for the clothing they wore—the uniforms designating their various occupations served to differentiate and identify them.

A world of Skinners on Skinner's world.

There had been problems, of course.

Long ago, before Dr. Togol began his work, they'd discussed the matter.

"One true clone," Dr. Togol said. "That's enough to aim for. One healthy facsimile of yourself is all you need."

Skinner shook his head. "Too risky. Suppose there's an accident? That would be the end of me."

"Very well. We'll arrange to keep extra cellular tissue alive, in reserve. Carefully stored and guarded, of course."

"Guarded?"

"But of course," Dr. Togol nodded. "This Eden, this satellite of yours, will need protection. And since you seem to be determined not to run it by computer, you're going to need personnel. Other people to do the work, keep things going, provide you with companionship. Surely you won't want to live forever if you must spend eternity alone."

Skinner frowned. "I don't trust people. Not as guards, not as employees, certainly not as friends."

"No one at all?"

"I trust myself," Skinner said. "So I want more clones. Enough to keep Eden going independently of any outsider."

"The whole satellite populated by nothing but Skinners?"

"Exactly."

"But you don't seem to understand. If the process succeeds and I produce more than one Skinner, they'll share everything. Not just bodies like yours, but minds—each personality will be identical. They'll have the same memories, right up to the moment that the cells are excised from your body."

"I understand that."

"Do you?" Dr. Togol shook his head. "Let's say I follow your instructions. Technically speaking, it's possible—if a single cloning is successful, then the rest would be successful too. All that would be involved is the additional expense of the process."

"Then there's no problem, is there?"

"I told you what the problem is. A thousand Skinners, exactly alike. Looking alike, thinking alike, feeling alike. And you—the present you, reproduced by cloning—would just be one of the many. Have you decided what job you want to perform on your new world once you've become immortal? Do you want to tend the power banks—would you like to unload supplies—do you think you'd enjoy working in the kitchens of the big house forever?"

"Certainly not!" Skinner snapped. "I want to be just what I am now."

"The boss. Top man. Mr. Big." Dr. Togol smiled, then sighed. "That's just the point. So will all the others. Every one of your counterparts will have the same desire, the same goal, the same drive to dominate, to control. Because they'll all have your exact brain and nervous system."

"Up to the time they are reborn, you might say?"

"Right."

"Then from that moment on, you'll institute a new program. A program of conditioning." Skinner nodded quickly. "There are techniques for that, I know. Sleep learning, deep hypnosis machines—the sort of thing psychologists use to alter criminal behavior. You'll plant memory blocks selectively."

"But I'd need an entire psychomedical center, completely staffed—"

"You'll have it. I want the whole procedure carried out right here on earth, before anyone is transported to Eden."

"I'm not sure. You're asking for the creation of a new race, each with a new personality. A Skinner who'll remember his past life but is now content to be merely a hydroponic gardener, a Skinner who'll be satisfied to live forever as an accountant, a Skinner willing to devote his entire endless existence as a repairman."

Skinner shrugged. "A difficult and complicated job, I know. But then you'll be working with a difficult and complicated personality—mine." He cleared his throat painfully before continuing. "Not that I'm unique. We're all far more complicated than we appear to be on the surface, you know that. Each human being is a bundle of conflicting impulses, some expressed, some suppressed. I know that there's a part of me which has always been close to nature, to the soil, to the cultivation and growth of life. I've buried that facet of my personality away since childhood but the memories are there. Find them and you'll have your gardeners, your farmers—yes, and your medical staff assistants too!

"Another part of me is fascinated even consciously today by facts and figures, the *minutiae* of mathematics. Isolate that aspect, condition it to full expression, and you'll get your accountant, and all the help you need to keep Eden running smoothly and systematically.

"I don't need to tell you that a great share of my early career was devoted to scientific research and invention. You won't have any problem developing mechanical-minded Skinners to staff power units, or even to drive transport vehicles.

"The reaches of the mind are infinite, Doctor. Exploit them properly and you'll have a working world—with all the petty authority roles filled by Skinners who have the urge to play policeman or foreman or supervisor—and all the menial tasks performed by Skinners who long to serve. Resurrect those specific traits and tendencies, intensify them, blot out all the memories which might conflict with them, and the rest is easy."

"Easy?" Dr. Togol scowled. "To brainwash them all?"

"All but one." Skinner's voice was crisp. "One will remain untouched, reproduced exactly and entirely as is. And that will be me."

The greyhaired, potbellied little medical scientist stared at Skinner for a long moment.

"You don't admit the possibility of any changes in yourself? The desirability of modifying some of your own personality pattern?"

"I don't think I'm perfect, if that's what you mean. But I'm satisfied with myself as I am. And as I will be, once you've carried out the plan."

Dr. Togol continued to stare. "You say you have learned to trust no one. If that's true—and I'm inclined to believe you—then how do you know you can trust me?"

"What do you mean?"

"You're going to die. We both know that. It's only a matter of time. The power to regenerate you through cloning is entirely in my hands. Suppose I don't go through with it?"

Skinner met Dr. Togol's stare. "You'll go through with it before I die. And long before I'm helpless and unable to issue orders, you'll be processing the clones as I've directed. I assure you I have every intention of staying alive until all the clones are ready for transportation to Eden."

"But you *will* die then," Togol insisted. "And there'll be the one clone you've chosen to represent yourself—the one you insist must remain unchanged. What makes you so sure I'll obey that directive after you're actually dead? I could use psychological techniques to modify your clone's personality then in any way I choose. What's to prevent me from making your clone my willing slave—so that I'd be the real master of this new world you created?"

"Curiosity," Skinner murmured. "You'll do exactly as I say because you're fanatically and completely curious about the outcome. No other man alive can provide you with the means and opportunity to carry through this cloning project. If the experiment succeeds you'll have made the greatest scientific breakthrough of all time—so you won't betray your trust by failure or refusal. And once you go that far, you won't be able to resist following through. Particularly when you come to realize that this is only the beginning."

"I don't understand."

"All my life I've moved forward from a position of strength, of self-confidence. And you know what I have achieved. I think I'm presently the wealthiest and most powerful individual in the galaxy.

"I'm a sick man now, but thanks to you I'm going to be well again. Not only well, but immortal. Consider the kind of confidence I'll possess once I'm free of illness, free forever from the fear of death. With my thrust we can go on to far greater concepts, far greater achievements—solve all the mysteries, shatter all the barriers, shake the stars!

"You can't afford to tamper with my mind because you'll want to be a part of it all—to see and to share. Right, doctor?"

Togol's glance faltered. He had no answer, because he knew it was true.

And it had been true.

The cloning was carried out just as Seward Skinner had planned it. And the psychological conditioning project which followed was properly performed too, even though in the end it proved to be far more complicated than anyone had imagined.

The final step involved recruiting a staff of several hundred technicians, highly skilled and specially schooled, then divided into psychomedical teams assigned to the individual clones as they were nurtured to full growth and emerged as functioning adult specimens. Under Dr. Togol's supervision these specialists created the programs for memory blocking, for shaping the personalities of each separate Skinner to fit him for his life role when he reached Eden.

After that the shuttling began.

Space transports, manned exclusively by Skinners trained for the task, brought other Skinners to the stony surface of the secret satellite. Additional Skinner-piloted transports convoyed and conveyed the seemingly endless supply of materials needed to transform the empty expanse of Eden into the world of Seward Skinner's dream.

The miniature city rose on the plain, the house went up on the hillside, the laboratory complex grew over the great vault below. And all of this, every step of the operation, was carried out in such strict, security guarded secrecy that no outsider ever suspected its existence.

As time went on the steps became part of a race—a race with death.

Skinner was dying. Only an act of incredible will kept him alive long enough to supervise the total destruction of the earthsite where the work had taken place.

Then he himself went to Eden with Dr. Togol, but not until he'd made arrangements to send up the entire psychomedical staff, intact, to the new laboratory complex there.

For this a final transport was arranged.

Skinner vividly remembered the evening he lay on his deathbed in the hillside house with Dr. Togol, awaiting the arrival of the transport.

Flickering forth in the darkened room, the media transmitter screened its shocking message. *Pressure failure and implosion beyond Pluto—transport totally destroyed—no survivors.*

"My God!" said Togol.

Then, in the dim light, he saw the smile on the face of the dying man. And heard the harsh, labored whisper.

"Did you really believe I'd ever allow any outsiders to come here—to pry, interfere—learn the secrets—carry the news back into other worlds?"

Togol stared at him. "Sabotaging a transport, murdering all those men! You can't possibly get away with it!"

"*Fait accompli.*" Skinner grimaced. "No one on board knew the true destination—they thought it was Rigel. And what happened will be recorded as an accident."

"Unless I choose to report it."

The dying man's features caricatured a smile. "You won't. Because there is a single detailed account of the whole scheme hidden away in my files. It implicates you as my accomplice, so if you speak you'll be signing your own death warrant."

"You forget that I can sign yours," Dr. Togol said. "Merely by letting nature take its course."

"If you let me die now, everything in my files will come to light. So you have no choice. You're going to go through with it—proceed with the final cloning that will reproduce me as I've ordered."

Togol took a deep breath. "So that's why you were so confident I'd never betray you! You weren't relying on my scientific curiosity—you'd planned this all along, to have a permanent hold on me."

"I told you I was a complex man." Skinner winced with pain. "Now it is time to make me a whole and healthy one. You'll start now—tonight."

It wasn't an order, merely a statement of fact.

And, factually, Dr. Togol had proceeded according to plan.

Seward Skinner was grateful for that, grateful that his new clone-born self evolved before his old body had actually died. Because if Togol had waited until then, the clone would have held the memory of Skinner's death. And that is a memory no man can bear.

As it was, the living tissue that was now Skinner had begun its growth process in the laboratory complex safely before the pain racked, rotting tissue of the body in the house ceased to function. Skinner was not aware of just when he had died; he was too busy learning how to live.

Working without a team of technicians was a great handicap, but Dr. Togol had overcome it quickly and efficiently—with the aid of other Skinners to whom he was able to impart rudimentary medical skills. Since then, of course, he had cloned an entire staff of Skinners for that purpose—Dr. Skinner, the psychotherapy chief; Dr. Skinner, the head surgeon; Dr. Skinner, the diagnostic specialist; and a dozen others.

"You see, we didn't need outsiders after all," the new Skinner told Togol, after it was over. "We're totally self-sustaining here. And when these bodies start to show signs of deterioration and function failure, new clones will replace them. Everyone's dream of true immortality, realized at last."

"Everyone's?" Dr. Togol shook his head. "Not mine."

"Then you're a fool," Skinner said. "You have the opportunity to clone yourself, live forever, just as I intend to. I've granted you that privilege. What more could you ask?"

"Freedom."

"But you're free here. You have the resources of the galaxy at your disposal—you can expand the lab unit indefinitely, go on to major research in other fields, just as I promised you. That cure for cancer they've been talking about for the past hundred years—don't you want to find it? You've implemented some marvelous memory blocking techniques already, but this is only the beginning of a whole new psychotherapy. You can build new personalities, reshape the human condition as you will—"

"As *you* will." Togol's smile was bitter. "This is your world. I want my own. The old world, with ordinary people, men—and women—"

"You know very well why I decided against women here," Skinner said. "They're not necessary for reproduction. Fortunately, at my age, the sexual impulse is no longer an imperative. So females would only complicate our existence, without serving any true function."

"Tenderness, compassion, understanding, companionship," Togol murmured. "All nonfunctional by your definition."

"Stereotype. Utter nonsense. Sentimentalization of a biological role which you and I have rendered obsolete."

"You've rendered everything obsolete," Togol told him. "Everything except the antlike activity of your clone colony—the warped and crippled partial personalities created to serve you."

"They're happy the way they are," Skinner said. "And it doesn't matter. What matters is that *I* haven't changed. I'm a whole man."

"Are you?" Dr. Togol's smile was mirthless. He nodded towards the house, gestured to include the terrace and the city below. "Everything you've built here, everything you've done, is a product of the most crippling defect of all—the fear of death."

"But all men are afraid to die."

"So afraid that they spend their entire lives just trying to avoid the realization of their own mortality?" Togol shook his head. "You know there's a vault underneath my laboratory. You know why it was built. You know what it contains. And yet your fear is so great that you won't even admit it exists."

"Take me there," Skinner said.

"You don't mean that."

"Come on. I'll show you I'm not frightened."

But he was.

Even before they reached the elevator Skinner started to tremble, and as they began their deep descent to the lower level he was shuddering uncontrollably.

"Cold down here," he muttered.

Dr. Togol nodded. "Temperature control," he said.

They left the elevator and walked along a dark corridor towards the steel-sheathed chamber set in stone. Security guard Skinner stood sentinel at the door and smiled a greeting as they approached. At Togol's order, he produced a key and opened the vault door.

Seward Skinner didn't look at him and he didn't want to look beyond the doorway.

But Dr. Togol had already entered and now there was no choice but to follow. Follow him into the dim light of the chill chamber—to the looming control banks that whined and whirred in the center of the room—to the tangled cluster of tubes and inputs which snaked down from all sides into a transparent glass cylinder.

Skinner stared through the shadows at the cylinder. It was shaped like a coffin, because it was a coffin; a coffin in which Seward Skinner saw—

Himself.

His own body; the wasted, shriveled body from which the clones had sprung, floating in the clear solution amid the coils and clamps and weblike wires tunneling through the glass covering to terminate in contact with frozen flesh.

"Not dead," Dr. Togol murmured. "Frozen in solution. The cryogenic process, preserving you in suspended animation—indefinitely—"

Skinner shuddered again and turned away. "Why?" he whispered. "Why didn't you let me die?"

"You wanted immortality."

"But I have it. With this new body, all the others."

"Flesh is vulnerable. Any accident can destroy it."

"You've stored more cell tissue. If anything happened to me as I am now, you could repeat the cloning."

"Only if your original body remains available for the process. It had to be preserved against such an emergency—alive."

Skinner forced himself to glance again at the corpse-like creature congealed in cold behind its crystal confines.

"It's not alive—it can't be—"

And yet he knew it was, knew that the cryogenic process had been developed for just that purpose. To maintain a minimum life force in hibernation against the time when medical science could arrest and eliminate its disease processes and develop techniques to thaw it out and successfully restore complete and conscious existence again.

Skinner realized this goal had never been achieved, but the possibility remained. Some day perhaps the methodology would be perfected and this thing might be resurrected—not as a clone, but as he had been. The original Skinner, alive once more and a rival to his present self.

"Destroy it," he said.

Dr. Togol stared at him. "You don't mean that. You can't—"

"Destroy it!"

Skinner turned and walked out of the vault.

Dr. Togol remained behind, and it was a long time before he returned to rejoin Skinner in his house on the surface. What he'd done there in the vault he did not say, and Skinner never inquired. The subject wasn't discussed again.

But since that night Skinner's relationship with Togol had never been quite the same. There was no more discussion of the future, of possible new projects and experiment. There was only a heightened awareness of tension, of waiting, an indefinable atmosphere of alienation. Dr. Togol spent more and more of his time within the laboratory complex, where he maintained separate living quarters of his own. And Skinner went his own way, alone.

Alone, yet not alone. For this was his world, and it was filled with his own people, created in his own image. *Thou shalt have no God but Skinner. And Skinner is His prophet.*

That was the commandment and the law. And if Dr. Togol chose not to abide by it—

Now Seward Skinner, walking the streets of his own city, came to the door of the museum.

Skinner, the chauffeur, waited outside, smiling in obedience at the order, and Skinner, the museum guard, nodded happily as Seward Skinner entered.

Skinner, the curator, greeted him, delighted at the sight of a visitor. No one ever came to the museum except his master—indeed, the whole notion of a museum was merely a quaint conceit, an archaicism from the distant past on earth.

But Seward Skinner had felt the need for such a place here; a storehouse and a showcase for the art and artifacts he'd accumulated in the past. And while he could have stocked it with the treasures and trophies gathered throughout the galaxy, he'd elected to exhibit only objects from earth. Obsolete objects at that—mementos and memorabilia representing ancient history. Here in the halls were the riches and relics of long ago and far away. Paintings from palaces, sculpture and statues from shrines; the jewels and jade and gorgeous gewgaws which had once represented royal tastes, rescued from regal tombs.

Skinner walked through the displays with scarcely a glance at its glories. Ordinarily he might have spent hours admiring the ancient television set, the library of printed books hermetically sealed in plexiglass, the slot machine, the reconstructed gas engine automobile in perfect running condition.

Today he went straight to remote room and indicated one of the items on display.

"Give me that."

The curator's polite smile masked perplexity, but he obeyed.

Then Skinner turned and retraced his steps. At the door the chauffeur waited to escort him back to the minimobile.

Driving back through the streets, Skinner smiled once more at the passersby and watched them as they went about their ways.

How could Togol call them crippled? They were happy in their work, their lives were fulfilled. Each had been conditioned to accept his lot without envy, competition or hostility. Thanks to their conditioning and the selective screening of memory patterns they seemed much more content than the Seward Skinner who surveyed them as he returned to his house on the hill.

But he too would be satisfied, and soon.

That evening he summoned Dr. Togol.

Seated on the terrace in the twilight, inhaling the synthetic scent of the simulated flowers, Skinner smiled a greeting at the scientist.

"Sit down," he said. "It's time we had a talk."

Togol nodded and sank into a chair with an audible sigh of effort.

"Tired?"

Togol nodded. "I've been quite busy lately."

"I know." Skinner twirled his brandy snifter. "Assembling data on the project here must be quite exhausting."

"It's important to have a complete record."

"You've put it all on microtape, haven't you? A single spool, small enough to be carried in a man's pocket. How very convenient."

Dr. Togol stiffened and sat upright.

Skinner's smile was serene. "Did you propose to smuggle it out? Or take it back yourself on the next transport shuttle to earth?"

"Who told you—"

Skinner shrugged. "It's obvious enough. Now that you've achieved the goal you want the glory. A triumphant return—your name and fame echoing throughout the galaxy—"

Togol frowned. "It's natural for you to think of it in terms of ego. But that's not the reason. You told me yourself before we started—this can be the most significant achievement in all time. The discovery must be shared, put to use for the benefit of others."

"I paid for the research. I funded the project. It's my property."

"No man has the right to withhold knowledge."

"It's my property," Skinner repeated.

"But I'm not." Dr. Togol rose.

Skinner's smile faded. "Suppose I refuse to let you go?"

"I wouldn't advise it."

"Threats?"

"A statement of fact." Togol met Skinner's stare. "Let me leave in peace. You have my word that your secret is safe. I'll share my findings but preserve your privacy. No one will ever learn the location of Eden."

"I'm not in the habit of making bargains."

"I realize that." Dr. Togol nodded. "So I've already taken certain precautions."

"What sort of precautions?" Skinner chuckled, enjoying the moment. "You forget—this is my world."

"You have no world." Togol faced him, frowning. "All this is merely a mirror maze. The ultimate end of the megalomaniac carried to its logical extreme. In the old days conquerors and kings surrounded themselves with portraits and paintings celebrating their triumphs, commissioned statues and raised pyramids as monuments to their vanity. Servants and slaves sung their praises, sycophants erected shrines to their divinity. You've done all that and more. But it won't last. No man is an island. The tallest temples topple, the most fawning followers go down into dust."

"Do you deny you've given me immortality?"

"I've given you what you want, what every man in search of power *really* wants—the illusion of his own omnipotence. And you're welcome to keep it." Dr. Togol nodded. "But if you try to stop me—"

"I intend to do just that." Seward Skinner's smile returned. "Now."

"Skinner! For God's sake—"

"Yes. For my sake."

Still smiling, Skinner reached into his jacket and brought forth the object he'd taken from the museum.

There was a flicker of flame in the twilight, a single sharp sound shattering the silence, and Dr. Togol fell with a bullet lodged between his eyes.

Skinner summoned Skinner, who scrubbed the tiny trickle of blood from the terrace. Two other Skinners removed the body.

And life went on.

It would always go on, now. Go on forever, free from outside interference. Skinner was safe on Skinner's world. Safe to make further plans.

Dr. Togol was right, of course. He *was* a megalomaniac, the fact must be faced. Skinner admitted that. Easy enough, because he wasn't a madman, merely a realist, and the realist admits the truth, which is that one's ego is all important. A simple fact to a complex man.

And even Togol hadn't realized how complex Skinner was. Complex enough to make further plans. He'd been thinking about it for a long time now.

Being immortal and independent here in a world of his own was only the beginning. Suppose the infinite resources of Seward Skinner's galactic complex were utilized now to the ultimate, inexorable end—the end of every other world?

It would take time, but he had eternity. It would take effort, but immortality never tires. There would be a way and a weapon, and eventually he would find both. Eventually the scheme would be implemented, and then in truth there would be nothing in the galaxy but God. Skinner, and only Skinner, forever and ever, amen.

Skinner sat on the terrace and stared out as darkness fell over the land. A vague plan was already taking shape in his mind—the keen, immortally conscious, eternally aware mind.

There was a way, a simple way. Skinner scientists would be pressed into service to carry out the details, and with his resources it was neither fantastic nor impossible. It could be in fact quite simple. Develop a mutant microorganism, an airborne virus impervious to immunization, then transmit it by shuttle to key points throughout the galaxy. Human life, animal life, vegetable life would perish forever in its wake. Forever and ever, amen.

To be the richest man in the world was nothing. To be the wisest, the strongest, the most powerful—this too was not enough. But to be the *only* man—forever—

Seward Skinner started to laugh.

And then, quite suddenly, his laughter shrilled into a scream.

All over his world, Skinner screamed. The sound echoed through the curator's quarters in the museum, rose from the streets where the security guards stood sentinel, burst from the chauffeur's sleeping lips, shrieked in chorus from each and every Skinner who found himself *down there.*

The Skinner on the terrace was down there, too. Down there where —a remnant of sanity recalled—Dr. Togol must have taken his precautions and his revenge. It was a simple thing he'd done, really.

He'd gone *down there,* to the vault where the original Seward Skinner floated in the icy solution which preserved him in hibernation. And all he'd done was to shut off the temperature controls.

Dr. Togol had lied about destroying the thing in the vault. He'd kept it alive, and now that it was thawing its consciousness returned—the original consciousness of the real Seward Skinner, waking in the black, bubbling vat to wheeze and gasp and choke its life away.

And because it was aware now, the clones were linked to that life and that awareness, sharing the shock and sensation as the artificial blocks vanished, so that all again were one.

In a moment the thing down there in the vault was dead. But not before all the Skinners felt its final agony—which would never be final for them. As clones, they were immortal.

Seward Skinner's scream blended with those of every other Skinner on Skinner's world. And they would continue.

Forever.

...and the power...

By RACHEL COSGROVE PAYES

May 9: Denton got word today of another healer, this one somewhere in the wilds of Tennessee. Hope it's not another one of those snake handlers. They give me the creeps. The last three we've tested have been duds—no measurable rays, and no cures, either. Our theory is shaping up better with each test we make. My turn to cut my hand, though. Don't look forward to that. With this miserable headache I've been getting so often lately, I don't look forward to much of anything.

May 15: Denton says spring is lovely in the Smokies. He has the trip planned for next week. A big revival starting then. How I hate these jaunts, and the ignoramuses we meet. If I ever had any religion, I've lost it going to these revivals. If just once I could convince one of these guys that he's a real scientific oddity—that only the true healers have these identifiable radiations coming from their hands—that they're born with it, and all the hallelujah hoopla is just showmanship. But they all try to convert me. I've made up my mind. This time, I'll do the converting, if this evangelist appears to have even a modicum of brains. Faith healers! Poor slobs, they could attribute their power to the devil for all I care. It's in their hands, no matter whom they give credit for it. Literally. Hope we can do more than just report the phenomenon. If only we could find out why just certain people give off these rays. Think of a clinic full of these authentic healers. We'd make the biggest splash medicine has seen in the last century. And if we could learn to reproduce it in others—I can see that Nobel prize with our names on it right now.

May 20: Cold and rainy here, but I shouldn't complain. Denton slipped on a wet brick sidewalk and broke his wrist. So he says there's no need for me to cut my thumb, to test this healer. He'll use the broken wrist. We'll wait until tomorrow night, as he's still dopey from having the wrist set. I don't think I'll go to tonight's service. My head's aching. Change in altitude, probably.

May 21: Bingo! A winner. This Stonestreet gave the highest readings we've ever had. When he called for the sick to come forward, and Denton turned on his wrist meter, I was skeptical. Stonestreet isn't the type we've found most places. Oh, he's the usual backwoods evangelistic type, in a way—but not so much Bible beating and shouting. Really rather impressive, the way he stands there, full of confidence in his power to heal. And why shouldn't he be confident? When he laid his hands on Denton's cast, the needle went right off the scale. Of course we have to wait until tomorrow to have the wrist x-rayed again, but Denton insists it's okay. Says he can tell by the way it feels. If so, then I'm going to work on this Stonestreet right away. Just once I intend to convince one of these poor goops that this is a true scientific phenomenon. If they like to dress it up in the trappings of religion, to draw a crowd, well, it's their business, I guess. But I can prove that the Bible mumbo-jumbo is just that. This Stonestreet impresses me as intelligent, although unschooled. This may be the time I pick a winner. If he'll just agree to cooperate with us, help us in our research, we'll have a paper ready by fall. And if he'll agree to let us open a clinic, we all can clean up financially.

May 22: Denton was right. The x-ray showed no break at all. The doc was all shook up about it, claimed that the technician must have goofed yesterday, but Denton and I know the truth. His wrist was broken, and now it's okay. I'm going to hear Stonestreet again tonight, then see if he won't talk with me.

May 23: Stonestreet–they should have called him Stonewall. Of course, I didn't expect him to believe me immediately–but that look on his face when I told him that his healing was due to a special kind of rays, similar to x-rays, which his hands put out. You'd have thought I'd called him every dirty name in the book the way he looked at me. Then it got worse. He began to pity me. It was laughable. Here I am, feeling sorry for him because he's so ignorant, and he's pitying me because I'm a heathen. I've got to admit that he's a persuasive cuss, but so am I. And I think I've hit on a clever plan for getting my message across to him. He thinks I need to be converted, so I'm going to play along with him. While he's converting me, I'll just do a bit of converting on my own. This is going to take some time, but it'll be worth it, if we can just get through to him that he'd be able to heal whether or not he prayed over us. From the time I spent with him tonight, I'm convinced that he has a lot of native intelligence, if we just can channel it properly.

Got to knock off this journal now. That headache's back again. Must remember to buy aspirin tomorrow.

May 29: I think we're finally getting through to Stonestreet. He has agreed to let us run some experiments with our equipment. And I've found, in conversing with him, that he has a great interest in science. He's just never applied it to himself, that's all. Doesn't realize that his healing is a genuine scientific phenomenon. If we can learn the origin of these rays, we'll be famous. After tonight's service, I'll set up a time tomorrow when he'll let us do experiments.

May 30: Had to do our work this afternoon, as Stonestreet gave the invocation at the Memorial Day services this morning. First we tested him cold. And got no readings. Didn't expect any, though. This is what we observed with Bishop White, and with Laramie Sue in Arizona last year. They seem to be able to turn the energy on and off. We'd explained to Stonestreet about the experiments; so when we got no needle fluctuation, he laughed, and said he'd known all along we were kidding him. His power was from the Lord Jesus, not from invisible rays in his hands. Then we asked him to heal a local kid who was covered with poison ivy, a systemic case, and he went into his prayer routine. This time the needle went off the scale, and the rash went off the kid. So Stonestreet insisted he'd proved his point, that his power was from the Divine. But Denton and I tried to get through to him that he, himself, willed that energy into his hands when he concentrated. The prayer as such was unnecessary. We tried to get him to agree to heal without praying, but he turned stubborn on us and refused. Left then, saying he'd pray for us. We needed it. I went to his healing service tonight, and he knew I was there. This time I didn't mention experiment. I just sat and watched. But we've planted the seed, now maybe it'll take root. Denton jokingly said I should let him cure my headache, but it'd be a daily job for him, I'm afraid.

June 5: Our experiments are working beyond our wildest hopes. Stonestreet is cooperating fully, now; and I think that Denton and I are finally getting through to him. Today he didn't quote scripture to us once. And he's been asking many good questions, for one who's had so little formal education. Today, when he left, he asked if we would lend him some books on science, books pertaining to our work. We explained that we were pioneering a new area, but we gave him some general things to read, to give him a background for what we're trying to do. I finally had to quit working on my notes this afternoon, because the lines were beginning to run together. One of these days I'll have my eyes checked. I may need reading glasses. Probably why my head is splitting most of the time.

June 6: I blacked out today. Denton's pretty worried, and insists that I take time out to go to Chattanooga to see a doctor he knows. He called and arranged an appointment for me for tomorrow. Wish I could spend the day with Stonestreet, instead. He's coming across, I think. He told me he'd sat up half the night thinking about what I've been saying about the healing rays in his hands—thinking, he said, not praying. When we first met him, every other word was God, or Jesus, or Bible, or prayer. Now he's beginning to think, to use his brain the way nature intended that it be used. I'd better get to bed. It's a long drive to Chattanooga tomorrow. Glad Denton's offered to go with me. After blacking out today, I'm hesitant about taking the wheel myself. Hope this doctor can pinpoint my trouble in a hurry. Once it's diagnosed properly for the scientific records, I'll let Stonestreet lay his hands on my poor aching head and make me one of my own case histories.

June 7: Dr. Loeb didn't say too much. He put me through my paces, asked a lot of questions, and said he wanted to do some tests. I'm to be admitted to the hospital tomorrow morning for a day or two. Denton seems worried, although why, I don't know. As I said to him, Stonestreet can do his healing bit on me. That may well be a scientific first in itself.

June 10: Inoperable brain tumor. For just a minute, when Dr. Loeb gave his verdict, I felt panicky. He didn't pull his punches. Says I have six weeks or perhaps a little longer. Then I remembered Stonestreet, and I actually laughed in poor Loeb's face. From the look he gave me, he thinks I've flipped. Denton's in a real sweat. He doesn't seem to have the faith in Stonestreet that I have, even after his broken wrist. He keeps saying, "But a brain tumor—that's different." Loeb wants me to stay here in the hospital. All I want is to get back to that wide place in the road that Stonestreet calls home. My head hurts all the time now, and my vision is very bad. Denton refuses to drive me, so I'm making arrangements for an ambulance to get me there.

June 12: I collapsed yesterday, and the ambulance crew refused to transport me. I've sent Denton to get Stonestreet and bring him here. Denton says Dr. Loeb may not allow the healer to see me, but I'll just say he's my spiritual advisor. No hospital in the country will keep out a man under those conditions. Loeb doesn't have to know why Stonestreet's here. Until after I'm healed, at any rate. Too doped up to write more tonight. Denton should be here tomorrow with Stonestreet.

June 13: Where's Denton? I've refused dope all day, so I'd be clear headed, but Denton's not come back, and there's been no word from him. I wanted to try to call through to see if I could catch him, but Stonestreet doesn't have a telephone.

June 14: Denton finally showed up at noon, looking like death warmed over. When I asked if he'd brought Stonestreet with him, he stalled. Finally he told me. Mrs. Stonestreet was alone at the house. She says that her husband told her he had an important decision to make, one which might alter the shape of his life. He was going out into the hills alone to meditate. When I asked Denton when she expected him back, he said, "Not for forty days." That's cutting it too fine for me. I've told Denton to get back there and locate Stonestreet if he has to ring in the State Police, or a sheriff's posse, or enlist every bloodhound in the state of Tennessee. I don't intend to die, not now, not with healing in a man's fingertips to get rid of this tumor for me.

June 21: A whole week, and no sign of Stonestreet. I told Denton that he must explain everything to Stonestreet's wife. Surely she has some idea of where he's gone. Forty days in the wilderness! Who does Stonestreet think he is, anyway, Jesus Christ? My eyes are so bad now that I can scarcely see to scribble in this journal.

June 28: Fourteen days, and no sign of Stonestreet. His wife finally agreed to go to the police, tell them the story. We have to have search parties comb the mountains for him. Forty days could be too late for me, I'm afraid.

July 4: Dependence Day for me. Dependence on narcotics. Where is Stonestreet?

July 14: Too sick to make entries. No Stonestreet. Denton's afraid something's happened to him, alone in the mountains. Doesn't say so, but I know him so well.

July 22: Thirty-eight days. Never found Stonestreet. I may not make it two more days. Nearly blind. Terrible pain.

July 23: Troopers finally located Stonestreet, explained the situation, and brought him out by helicopter. He walked into my room, big smile on his face, and announced, "You convinced me. *I* can heal." He held up those wonderful, life-giving hands and grinned. "As you kept telling me, it's those rays in my hands—not the religion. I fasted, and prayed, and read those books you loaned me, and thought. I finally realized that my skill is a gift, all right—a gift of nature. I'm with you scientists all the way, now." Just hearing him say this made my suffering worthwhile. Now Denton and I can begin to plan our clinic. Then Stonestreet apologized for allowing me to suffer and laid his hands on me. Tomorrow—by tomorrow I should be well again. But right now I'm too doped up to feel the difference. Just writing this is an effort.

July 24: No improvement. Stonestreet laid his hands on my head again today.

July 25: I can't hold out much longer. Stonestreet's worried, I can tell. I keep failing. Dr. Loeb is grave. Grave. Bad word.

July 26: Made Denton bring the testing equipment here. Stonestreet laid his hands on my head, but we got no reading on the meter. There are now no rays in his hands. Well, I got what I wanted. In convincing a healer that his power wasn't from God, I succeeded far beyond my wildest expectations.

caught in the organ draft

By ROBERT SILVERBERG

LOOK THERE, Kate, down by the promenade. Two splendid seniors, walking side by side near the water's edge. They radiate power, authority, wealth, assurance. He's a judge, a senator, a corporation president, no doubt, and she's—what?—a professor emeritus of international law, let's say. There they go toward the plaza, moving serenely, smiling, nodding graciously to passersby. How the sunlight gleams in their white hair! I can barely stand the brilliance of that reflected aura: it blinds me, it stings my eyes. What are they—eighty, ninety, a hundred years old? At this distance they seem much younger—they hold themselves upright, their backs are straight, they might pass for being only fifty or sixty. But I can tell. Their confidence, their poise, mark them for what they are. And when they were nearer I could see their withered cheeks, their sunken eyes. No cosmetics can hide that. These two are old enough to be our great-grandparents. They were well past sixty before we were even born, Kate. How superbly their bodies function! But why not? We can guess at their medical histories. She's had at least three hearts, he's working on his fourth set of lungs, they apply for new kidneys every five years, their brittle bones are reinforced with hundreds of skeletal snips from the arms and legs of hapless younger folk, their dimming sensory apparatus is aided by countless nerve grafts obtained the same way, their ancient arteries are freshly sheathed with sleek teflon. Ambulatory assemblages of second-hand human parts, spiced here and there with synthetic or mechanical organ substitutes, that's all they are. And what am I, then, or you? Nineteen years old and vulnerable. In their eyes I'm nothing but a ready stockpile of healthy organs, waiting to serve their needs. Come here, son. What a fine strapping young man you are! Can you spare a kidney for me? A lung? A choice little segment of intestine? Ten centimeters of your ulnar nerve? I need a few pieces of you, lad. You won't deny a distinguished elder leader like me what I ask, will you? *Will you?*

Today my draft notice, a small crisp document, very official looking, came shooting out of the data slot when I punched for my morning mail. I've been expecting it all spring: no surprise, no shock, actually rather an anticlimax now that it's finally here. In six weeks I am to report to Transplant House for my final physical exam—only a formality, they wouldn't have drafted me if I didn't already rate top marks as organ reservoir potential—and then I go on call. The average call time is about two months. By autumn they'll be carving me up. Eat, drink, and be merry, for soon comes the surgeon to my door.

A straggly band of senior citizens is picketing the central headquarters of the League for Bodily Sanctity. It's a counterdemonstration, an anti-anti-transplant protest, the worst kind of political statement, feeding on the ugliest of negative emotions. The demonstrators carry glowing signs that say:

BODILY SANCTITY—OR BODILY SELFISHNESS?

And:

YOU OWE YOUR LEADERS YOUR VERY LIVES

And:

LISTEN TO THE VOICE OF EXPERIENCE

The picketers are low-echelon seniors, barely across the qualifying line, the ones who can't really be sure of getting transplants. No wonder they're edgy about the league. Some of them are in wheelchairs and some are encased right up to the eyebrows in portable life support systems. They croak and shout bitter invective and shake their fists. Watching the show from an upper window of the league building, I shiver with fear and dismay. These people don't just want my kidneys or my lungs. They'd take my eyes, my liver, my pancreas, my heart, anything they might happen to need.

I talked it over with my father. He's forty-five years old—too old to have been personally affected by the organ draft, too young to have needed any transplants yet. That puts him in a neutral position, so to speak, except for one minor factor: his transplant status is 5-G. That's quite high on the eligibility list, not the top priority class but close enough. If he fell ill tomorrow and the Transplant Board ruled that his life would be endangered if he didn't get a new heart or lung or kidney, he'd be given one practically immediately. Status like that simply has to influence his objectivity on the whole organ issue. Anyway, I told him I was planning to appeal and maybe even to resist. "Be reasonable," he said, "be rational, don't let your emotions run away with you. Is it worth jeopardizing your whole future over a thing like this? After all, not everybody who's drafted loses vital organs."

"Show me the statistics," I said. "Show me."

He didn't know the statistics. It was his impression that only about a quarter or a fifth of the draftees actually got an organ call. That tells you how closely the older generation keeps in touch with the situation —and my father's an educated man, articulate, well informed. Nobody over the age of thirty-five that I talked to could show me any statistics. So I showed them. Out of a league brochure, it's true, but based on certified National Institute of Health reports. Nobody escapes. They always clip you, once you qualify. The need for young organs inexorably expands to match the pool of available organpower. In the long run they'll get us all and chop us to bits. That's probably what they want, anyway. To rid themselves of the younger members of the species, always so troublesome, by cannibalizing us for spare parts, and recycling us, lung by lung, pancreas by pancreas, through their own deteriorating bodies.

Fig. 4. On March 23, 1964, this dog's own liver was removed and replaced with the liver of a non-related mongrel donor. The animal was treated with azathioprine for four months and all therapy then stopped. He remains in perfect health 6–⅔ years after transplantation.

The war goes on. This is, I think, its fourteenth year. Of course they're beyond the business of killing now. They haven't had any field engagements since '93 or so, certainly—one since the organ draft legislation went into effect. The old ones can't afford to waste precious young bodies on the battlefield. So robots wage our territorial struggles for us, butting heads with a great metallic clank, laying land mines and twitching their sensors at the enemy's mines, digging tunnels beneath his screens, et cetera, et cetera. Plus, of course, the quasi-military activity—economic sanctions, third-power blockades, propaganda telecasts beamed as overrides from merciless orbital satellites, and stuff like that. It's a subtler war than the kind they used to wage: nobody dies. Still, it drains national resources. Taxes are going up again this year, the fifth or sixth year in a row, and they've just slapped a special Peace Surcharge on all metal-containing goods, on account of the copper shortage. There once was a time when we could hope that our crazy old leaders would die off or at least retire for reasons of health, stumbling away to their country villas with ulcers or shingles or scabies or scruples and allowing new young peacemakers to take office. But now they just go on and on, immortal and insane, our senators, our cabinet members, our generals, our planners. And their war goes on and on too, their absurd, incomprehensible, diabolical, self-gratifying war.

I know people my age or a little older who have taken asylum in Belgium or Sweden or Paraguay or one of the other countries where Bodily Sanctity laws have been passed. There are about twenty such countries, half of them the most progressive nations in the world and half of them the most reactionary. But what's the sense of running away? I don't want to live in exile. I'll stay here and fight.

Naturally they don't ask a draftee to give up his heart or his liver or some other organ essential to life, say his medulla oblongata. We haven't yet reached that stage of political enlightenment at which the government feels capable of legislating fatal conscription. Kidneys and lungs, the paired organs, the dispensable organs, are the chief targets so far. But if you study the history of conscription over the ages you see that it can always be projected on a curve rising from rational necessity to absolute lunacy. Give them a fingertip, they'll take an arm. Give them an inch of bowel, they'll take your guts. In another fifty years they'll be drafting hearts and stomachs and maybe even brains, mark my words; let them get the technology of brain transplants together and nobody's skull will be safe. It'll be human sacrifice all over again. The only difference between us and the Aztecs is one of method: we have anesthesia, we have antisepsis and asepsis, we use scalpels instead of obsidian blades to cut out the hearts of our victims.

MEANS OF OVERCOMING THE HOMOGRAFT REACTION

The pathway that has led from the demonstration of the immuno-

logical nature of the homograft reaction and its universality to the development of relatively effective but by no means completely satisfactory means of overcoming it for therapeutic purposes is an interesting one that can only be touched upon very briefly. The year 1950 ushered in a new era in transplantation immunobiology in which the discovery of various means of weakening or abrogating a host's response to a homograft—such as sublethal whole body x-irradiation, or treatment with certain adrenal corti-costeroid hormones, notably cortisone—began to influence the direction of the mainstream of research and engender confidence that a workable clinical solution might not be too far off. By the end of the decade powerful immuno-suppressive drugs, such as 6-mercaptopurine, had been shown to be capable of holding in abeyance the reactivity of dogs to renal homografts, and soon afterwards this principle was successfully extended to man.

Is my resistance to the draft based on an ingrained abstract distaste for tyranny in all forms or rather on the mere desire to keep my body intact? Could it be both, maybe? Do I need an idealistic rationalization at all? Don't I have an inalienable right to go through my life wearing my own native-born kidneys?

The law was put through by an administration of old men. You can be sure that all laws affecting the welfare of the young are the work of doddering moribund ancients afflicted with angina pectoris, atherosclerosis, prolapses of the infundibulum, fulminating ventricles, and dilated viaducts. The problem was this: not enough healthy young people were dying of highway accidents, successful suicide attempts, diving board miscalculations, electrocutions, and football injuries; therefore there was a shortage of transplantable organs. An effort to restore the death penalty for the sake of creating a steady supply of state-controlled cadavers lost out in the courts. Volunteer programs of organ donation weren't working out too well, since most of the volunteers were criminals who signed up in order to gain early release from prison: a lung reduced your sentence by five years, a kidney got you three years off, and so on. The exodus of convicts from the jails under this clause wasn't so popular among suburban voters. Meanwhile there was an urgent and mounting need for organs; a lot of important seniors might in fact die if something didn't get done fast. So a coalition of senators from all four parties rammed the organ draft measure through the upper chamber in the face of a filibuster threat from a few youth-oriented members. It had a much easier time in the House of Representatives, since nobody in the House ever pays much attention to the text of a bill up for a vote, and word had been circulated on this one that if it passed, everybody over sixty-five who had any political pull at all could count on living twenty or thirty extra years, which to a representative means a crack at ten to fifteen extra terms of office. Naturally there have been court challenges, but what's the use? The average age of the eleven justices of the Supreme Court is seventy-eight. They're human and mortal. They need our flesh. If they throw out the organ draft now, they're signing their own death warrants.

For a year and a half I was the chairman of the antidraft campaign on our campus. We were the sixth or seventh local chapter of the League for Bodily Sanctity to be organized in this country, and we were real activists. Mainly we would march up and down in front of the draft board offices carrying signs proclaiming things like:

KIDNEY POWER

And:

A MAN'S BODY IS HIS CASTLE

And:

THE POWER TO CONSCRIPT ORGANS IS THE POWER TO DESTROY LIVES

We never went in for the rough stuff, though, like bombing organ transplant centers or hijacking refrigeration trucks. Peaceful agitation, that was our motto. When a couple of our members tried to swing us to a more violent policy, I delivered an extemporaneous two-hour speech arguing for moderation. Naturally I was drafted the moment I became eligible.

"I can understand your hostility to the draft," my college advisor said. "It's certainly normal to feel queasy about surrendering important organs of your body. But you ought to consider the countervailing advantages. Once you've given an organ you get a 6-A classification, Preferred Recipient, and you remain forever on the 6-A roster. Surely you realize that this means that if you ever need a transplant yourself, you'll automatically be eligible for one, even if your other personal and professional qualifications don't lift you to the optimum level. Suppose your career plans don't work out and you become a manual laborer, for instance. Ordinarily you wouldn't rate even a first look if you developed heart disease, but your Preferred Recipient status would save you. You'd get a new lease on life, my boy."

I pointed out the fallacy inherent in this. Which is that as the number of draftees increases, it will come to encompass a majority or even a totality of the population, and eventually everybody will have 6-A Preferred Recipient status by virtue of having donated, and the term Preferred Recipient will cease to have any meaning. A shortage of transplantable organs would eventually develop as each past donor stakes his claim to a transplant when his health fails, and in time they'd have to arrange the Preferred Recipients by order of personal and professional achievement anyway, for the sake of arriving at some kind of priorities within the 6-A class, and we'd be right back where we are now.

Fig. 7. The course of a patient who received antilymphocyte globulin (ALG) before and for the first four months after renal homotransplantation. The donor was an older brother. There was no early rejection. Prednisone therapy was started forty days postoperatively. Note the insidious onset of late rejection after cessation of globulin therapy. This was treated by a moderate increase in the maintenance doses of steroids. This delayed complication occurred in only two of the first twenty recipients of intrafamilial homografts who were treated with

ALG. It has been seen with about the same low frequency in subsequent cases. (By permission of Surg. Gynec. Obstet. *126 (1968): p. 1023.)*

❧

So I went down to Transplant House today, right on schedule, to take my physical. A couple of my friends thought I was making a tactical mistake by reporting at all; if you're going to resist, they said, resist at every point along the line. Make them drag you in for the physical. In purely idealistic (and ideological) terms I suppose they're right. But there's no need yet for me to start kicking up a fuss. Wait till they actually say, "We need your kidney, young man." Then I can resist, if resistance is the course I ultimately choose. (Why am I wavering? Am I afraid of the damage to my career plans that resisting might do? Am I not entirely convinced of the injustice of the entire organ draft system? I don't know. I'm not even sure that I *am* wavering. Reporting for your physical isn't really a sellout to the system.) I went, anyway. They tapped this and x-rayed that and peered into the other thing. Yawn, please. Bend over, please. Cough, please. Hold out your left arm, please. They marched me in front of a battery of diagnostat machines and I stood there hoping for the red light to flash—*tilt,* get out of here!—but I was, as expected, in perfect physical shape, and I qualified for call. Afterward I met Kate and we walked in the park and held hands and watched the glories of the sunset and discussed what I'll do, when and if the call comes. *If?* Wishful thinking, boy!

❧

If your number is called you become exempt from military service, and they credit you with a special $750 tax deduction every year. Big deal.

❧

Another thing they're very proud of is the program of voluntary donation of unpaired organs. This has nothing to do with the draft, which

—thus far, at least—requisitions only paired organs, organs that can be spared without loss of life. For the last twelve years it's been possible to walk into any hospital in the United States and sign a simple release form allowing the surgeons to slice you up. Eyes, lungs, heart, intestines, pancreas, liver, anything, you give it all to them. This process used to be known as suicide in a simpler era and it was socially disapproved, especially in times of labor shortages. Now we have a labor surplus, because even though our population growth has been fairly slow since the middle of the century, the growth of labor-eliminating mechanical devices and processes has been quite rapid, even exponential. Therefore to volunteer for this kind of total donation is considered a deed of the highest social utility, removing as it does a healthy young body from the overcrowded labor force and at the same time providing some elder statesman with the assurance that the supply of vital organs will not unduly diminish. Of course, you have to be crazy to volunteer, but there's never been any shortages of lunatics in our society.

If you're not drafted by the age of twenty-one, through some lucky fluke, you're safe. And a few of us do slip through the net, I'm told. So far there are more of us in the total draft pool than there are patients in need of transplants. But the ratios are changing rapidly. The draft legislation is still relatively new. Before long they'll have drained the pool of eligible draftees, and then what? Birth rates nowadays are low; the supply of potential draftees is finite. But death rates are even lower; the demand for organs is essentially infinite. I can give you only one of my kidneys, if I am to survive; but you, as you live on and on, may require more than one kidney transplant. Some recipients may need five or six sets of kidneys or lungs before they finally get beyond hope of repair at age seventy-one or so. As those who've given organs come to requisition organs later on in life, the pressure on the under-twenty-one group will get even greater. Those in need of transplants will come to outnumber those who can donate organs, and everybody in the pool will get clipped. And then? Well, they could lower the draft age to seventeen or sixteen or even fourteen. But even that's only a short-term solution. Sooner or later, there won't be enough spare organs to go around.

Will I stay? Will I flee? Will I go to court? Time's running out. My call is sure to come up in another few weeks. I feel a tickling sensation in my back, now and then, as though somebody's quietly sawing at my kidneys.

Cannibalism. At Chou-kou-tien, Dragon Bone Hill, twenty-five miles southwest of Peking, paleontologists excavating a cave early in the twentieth century discovered the fossil skulls of Peking Man, *Pithecanthropus pekinensis*. The skulls had been broken away at the base, which led Franz Weidenreich, the director of the Dragon Bone Hill digs, to speculate that Peking Man was a cannibal who had killed his own kind, extracted the brains of his victims through openings in the base of their skulls, cooked and feasted on the cerebral meat—there were hearths and fragments of charcoal at the site—and left the skulls behind in the cave as trophies. To eat your enemy's flesh: to absorb his skills, his strengths, his knowledge, his achievements, his virtues. It took mankind five hundred thousand years to struggle upward from cannibalism. But we never lost the old craving, did we? There's still easy comfort to gain by devouring those who are younger, stronger, more agile than you. We've improved the techniques, is all. And so now they eat us raw, the old ones, they gobble us up, organ by throbbing organ. Is that really an improvement? At least Peking Man cooked his meat.

Our brave new society, where all share equally in the triumphs of medicine, and the deserving senior citizens need not feel that their merits and prestige will be rewarded only by a cold grave—we sing its praises all the time. How pleased everyone is about the organ draft! Except, of course, a few disgruntled draftees.

The ticklish question of priorities. Who gets the stockpiled organs? They have an elaborate system by which hierarchies are defined. Supposedly a big computer drew it up, thus assuring absolute godlike impartiality. You earn salvation through good works: accomplishments in career and benevolence in daily life win you points that nudge you up the ladder until you reach one of the high-priority classifications, 4-G or better. No doubt the classification system is impartial and is administered justly. But is it rational? Whose needs does it serve? In 1943, during World War II, there was a shortage of the newly discovered drug penicillin among the American military forces in North Africa. Two groups of soldiers were most in need of its benefits: those who were suffering from infected battle wounds and those who had contracted venereal disease. A junior medical officer, working from self-evident moral principles, ruled that the wounded heroes were more deserving of treatment than the self-indulgent syphilitics. He was overruled by the medical officer in charge, who observed that the VD cases could be restored to active duty more quickly, if treated; besides, if they remained untreated they served as vectors of further infection. Therefore he gave them the penicillin and left the wounded groaning on their beds of pain. The logic of the battlefield, incontrovertible, unassailable.

The great chain of life. Little creatures in the plankton are eaten by larger ones, and the greater plankton falls prey to little fishes, and little fishes to bigger fishes, and so on up to the tuna and the dolphin and the shark. I eat the flesh of the tuna and I thrive and flourish and grow fat, and store up energy in my vital organs. And am eaten in turn by the shriveled wizened senior. All life is linked. I see my destiny.

In the early days rejection of the transplanted organ was the big problem. Such a waste! The body failed to distinguish between a beneficial though alien organ and an intrusive, hostile microorganism. The mechanism known as the immune response was mobilized to drive out the invader. At the point of invasion enzymes came into play, a brush fire war designed to rip down and dissolve the foreign substances. White corpuscles poured in via the circulatory system, vigilant phagocytes on the march. Through the lymphatic network came antibodies, high-powered protein missiles. Before any technology of organ grafts could be developed, methods had to be devised to suppress the immune response. Drugs, radiation treatment, metabolic shock—one way and another, the organ rejection problem was long ago conquered. I can't conquer my draft rejection problem. Aged and rapacious legislators, I reject you and your legislation.

My call notice came today. They'll need one of my kidneys. The usual request. "You're lucky," somebody said at lunchtime. "They might have wanted a lung."

Kate and I walk into the green glistening hills and stand among the blossoming oleanders and corianders and frangipani and whatever. How good it is to be alive, to breathe this fragrance, to show our bodies to the bright sun! Her skin is tawny and glowing. Her beauty makes me weep. She will not be spared. None of us will be spared. I go first, then she, or is it she ahead of me? Where will they make the incision? Here, on her smooth rounded back? Here, on the flat taut belly? I can see the high priest standing over the altar. At the first blaze of dawn his shadow falls across her. The obsidian knife that is clutched in his upraised hand has a terrible fiery sparkle. The choir offers up a discordant hymn to the god of blood. The knife descends.

My last chance to escape across the border. I've been up all night, weighing the options. There's no hope of appeal. Running away leaves a bad taste in my mouth. Father, friends, even Kate, all say stay, stay, stay, face the music. The hour of decision. Do I really have a choice? I have no choice. When the time comes, I'll surrender peacefully.

I report to Transplant House for conscriptive donative surgery in three hours.

After all, he said coolly, what's a kidney? I'll still have another one, you know. And if that one malfunctions, I can always get a replacement. I'll have Preferred Recipient status, 6-A, for what that's worth. But I won't settle for my automatic 6-A. I know what's going to happen to the priority system; I'd better protect myself. I'll go into politics. I'll climb. I'll attain upward mobility out of enlightened self-interest, right? Right. I'll become so important that society will owe me a thousand transplants. And one of these years I'll get that kidney back. Three or four kidneys, fifty kidneys, as many as I need. A heart or two. A few lungs. A pancreas, a spleen, a liver. They won't be able to refuse me anything. I'll show them. I'll show them. I'll out-senior the seniors. There's your Bodily Sanctity activist for you, eh? I suppose I'll have to resign from the league. Goodbye, idealism. Goodbye, moral superiority. Goodbye, kidney. Goodbye, goodbye, goodbye.

It's done. I've paid my debt to society. I've given up unto the powers that be my humble pound of flesh. When I leave the hospital in a couple of days, I'll carry a card testifying to my new 6-A status.

Top priority for the rest of my life.

Why, I might live for a thousand years.

a sense of difference

By PAMELA SARGENT

And the Lord said unto Cain, Where is Abel thy brother? And he said, I know not: am I my brother's keeper?

Genesis 5:9

As Jim Swenson left the brightly lit doorway and walked outside, the shadows embraced him, hiding him from the girl he knew was watching him. He looked back, saw her raise an arm. Her face was hidden. She was a black shape outlined by the lights behind her. "Moira," a voice called to her from inside the dormitory, and she disappeared.

Jim walked toward the path leading through the wooded area around the dormitory, then stopped and looked back. The circular building was surrounded on three sides by trees and faced a large courtyard. Other circular dormitories, several stories high, overlooked the courtyard; beyond them, Jim could see, in the distance, the tall towers that housed the library and various research facilities of the university.

His birthplace was among the towers.

Jim turned and walked on through the woods. The shadows beneath the trees shielded him from the moon, the moon where scientists lived and labored in an attempt to carry on the work of his father, Paul Swenson.

Father. Paul had been closer than that.

They had buried Paul two years before, and left the gravesite, Jim holding the arm of his sister Kira, his three brothers following closely behind. Jim had looked up from the ground and seen them, as he knew he would, crowded in a herd a short distance away, cameras aimed at Jim and those with him. The newsmen did not have to come close to him in order to record accurately the grief written on his face; their equipment would record every detail of his sorrow and transmit it to a billion newsfax sheets and millions of large vision screens. The newsmen had huddled in the distance, ready to swoop.

He thought of Moira.

"A newsfax man came around," Moira had said, her black eyes smiling at Jim. "I guess someone told him we were seeing each other, and he wanted a personal story or something, what it's like to go with a guy who . . ."

"What did you tell him?" Jim asked, grabbing her arm. Moira looked at him, her eyes wide.

"Why, nothing," she said. "I have better things to do than discuss my personal life with the press."

He clenched his fist. "Why can't they leave me alone?" Moira reached over and took his arm.

"I guess," she said, "it'll be a long time before a clone has a private life." She had said it gently. He had reacted angrily, slamming his fist against a small table in her room and knocking over a small sculpture of a cat. The sculpture crashed to the floor and his stomach constricted, his muscles tensed.

Moira had been angry. He knew her mother had sculpted the cat for her years ago. Her voice had grown harsh, her sharp words had rained down on Jim.

"It was a lousy sculpture," he said to her. It was the wrong thing to say to Moira, who was already overly sensitive about her mother's second-rate abilities as an artist. Her black eyes had narrowed, the skin across the high cheek-bones had grown taut.

"So," Moira hissed, "she's not a good sculptor. She tries. At least she isn't an egomaniac, convinced of her great worth, her invaluable abilities; she never needed to see five duplicates of herself around before she could feel secure." She leaned over Jim, her black hair brushing his face. He looked away and kept picking up the broken pieces. "She wasn't *like* the great Paul Swenson."

Jim Swenson, one of the five duplicates of Paul Swenson, reached the end of the path through the forest and stopped at the edge of the university campus. He turned and walked along the edge of the bicycle path near the road which wound past the houses surrounding the campus.

Duplicates.

The wind breathed softly, rustling the leaves over his head. The trees nodded.

Duplicates of Paul Swenson. The wind hurried past him and was gone, leaving behind grassy odors.

Egomaniac. But the Paul Jim had known was a gentle man, almost self-effacing. Paul had not been content to lurk behind his studies, but had written about them, trying to communicate what he had learned to as many as possible. When Paul's friend Hidehiko Takamura, an embryologist, had approached him, telling him that it was possible to make an attempt at cloning human beings, Paul had consented to the use of his genetic material; he had wanted children, but had lost his beloved wife years before. Paul had only wanted to help humanity by perpetuating, in five new people, any abilities he might have that could be of service. So Jim had always thought. Yet it was at least possible that Paul might have been lured by dreams of a new and unique kind of immortality, or by an inner conviction that Paul Swenson was worthy of being reproduced, in exact detail and duplication, five times. The line between a sense of personal worth and megalomania might be very thin. Paul Swenson had been admired and honored; at the time of his death in a monorail accident, Jim had begun to sense the attitudes of fear and scepticism that colored the feelings many people had about Paul.

He had thought that Moira, at least, knew better. But she had not known Paul, and could only make judgments based on what she had heard or seen about him.

But she knows me, Jim thought, couldn't she tell that Paul wouldn't be like that? He sighed, and moved closer to the edge of the path as two cyclists passed him. He considered the problem again. Am I Paul? he asked himself. Paul had been near fifty when his five motherless children were removed from artificial wombs and presented to a startled world. The application of cloning to human beings was made illegal shortly afterward, and the artificial womb could be used only in hospitals to aid children born prematurely. Paul had lived with the five as a father, aiding and teaching them; what had he been like before that? What had he been like at twenty, Jim wondered, and his stomach contracted at the thought. I might be living his life over again, he thought, perhaps all of us are. He saw his brothers: Ed retreating from all social contact with others; Mike and his desire to leave all of them and forget his origins; Al and his obsession with study, afraid that he would not be able to measure up to Paul's achievements. He thought of Kira as well, hovering over them, concerned with their problems. Perhaps not, Jim thought, maybe she only thinks she *should* worry, and would rather retreat to her own world. Maybe Paul had gone through the same thing. Jim considered what he had heard about Paul's youth from old friends, and dismissed it. People edit their pasts, he knew, and remembered what fitted their notions of themselves. There was no way of telling what Paul had really felt.

Jim left the bicycle path and turned down the narrow road that led to his house. All five of them had remained in it after Paul's death. They had lived in it all their lives. It was practical, was near the university, was comfortable and roomy, but was haunted by Paul's ghost, Jim felt, watching all of them. He thought of Paul, standing in the house observing them, perhaps with concern, perhaps laughing as he saw them play out his own youth, his own mistakes, seeing his own soul taking up residence in the five bodies, genetically identical to his own.

The house was at the end of the road, its unpainted wooden planks blending with the small grove of trees around it. The inside of the house had been furnished eclectically, with large overstuffed chairs and couches contrasting with modern appliances. The library was a mixture of hardcover books and microfilm. Jim walked up to the front door, hesitated, then opened it slowly and entered the house.

He stood in the living room and watched as the four turned to face him: Al, thick brown hair to his shoulders; Ed, clean-shaven with hair cropped to his skull; Mike, pulling at his mustache; and Kira, with the same face feminized. Four sets of green eyes, copies of his own, looked at him and asked the same unspoken question: *are you all right, Jim?*

"Jim?" said Kira. His brothers still watched.

Jim turned and fled to his room.

Jim sat in Dr. Valois' office, feet propped on her desk, weaving images for her, speaking about portions of dreams, reaching into his pocket for a scrap of poetry he had jotted down to work on later. Emma Valois looked at him from her side of the desk, head nodding at intervals, blue eyes gazing at him steadily. He continued to weave his verbal tapestry, trying to ignore the anxiety that was gnawing at him, and the psychiatrist continued to nod.

Dr. Valois had been involved in the project that produced the clones, and had observed their psychological development for as long as Jim could remember. I guess they thought we'd need a psychiatrist, he thought, they expected us to be freaks. He read the poetry to Dr. Valois, and continued to avoid speaking about the feeling of despair that had brought him to the office. He could not bring himself to express it in words. He put the paper back in his pocket. Dr. Valois nodded.

Jim removed his feet from the desk and stood up. "I've got some research to do. In the library," he mumbled.

"You have nothing else to say?"

"No." He ran from the office, slowed down in the hallway and moved toward the elevator. He stepped into it automatically, jostling a man who was standing in the corner.

He was in Moira's room. "I love you," he said to her, reaching for her hand, and she turned from him. His brother Mike was standing at the door. Moira walked toward him and left Jim sitting at the desk.

Jim turned off the automated highway, took manual control of his car. He accelerated until the surrounding scenery was a blur, then quickly turned off the road, felt the car hurtle into nothingness. He reached out to death, and began to fall into a deep sleep.

He was walking across the campus, alone, as the newsfax man approached. "How about an interview, give me an exclusive, and I'll make it worth your while." The reporter's facial features were a blur. "What's it like to be a clone? Do you feel funny with four people around just like you? Can your friends tell you apart?" Jim grabbed the reporter's tape recorder and smashed it over the man's head.

"Jim," Moira's voice said. He looked around, startled. "Jim." He was standing just outside the elevator, and saw Moira coming toward him, her aqua sari fluttering at her ankles. He took her arm and walked through the lobby with her and then outside. The spring rain had stopped and the air smelled fresh.

"I must have said Jim five times," said Moira. "You looked like you were ready to kill somebody." They continued walking through the courtyard, surrounded on all sides by high silvery towers housing offices, research facilities and broadcasting studios. Few of the thousands of students were around; most of them were either doing research and lab work or were in their rooms, watching and listening to lectures.

"Just thinking about things," said Jim. "I guess . . ." he paused, feeling uneasy, and looked around the courtyard. All he saw were groups of students and faculty going about their business. "I guess," he went on, "I should go home and dial my Sci and Sym lectures, I'm about three lectures behind."

Moira shrugged. "It's an easy course," she said. Jim knew she had not thought much of the Science and Symbolism course, and had chosen to study literature that either did not deal with science at all, or only dealt with it peripherally. She did not care for science, and had never progressed beyond the basic courses recommended to all students. Jim glanced at Moira, thought he saw contempt in her eyes. Contempt for him? Contempt for Paul Swenson? Contempt for all of the biologists who had produced him?

"You can dial the lectures in my room," said Moira, "if you want."

Jim did not want to dial them at all. Inertia draped itself over him, and he saw himself continue through the courtyard, past the buildings, through the wooded areas, past the dormitories . . .

Moira saw the group before he did. She pulled at his arm and he saw a group of five teenagers being shown around the courtyard by a tall black man. She waved at the man. "Hey, Walt!" she shouted. The tall man waved back. "That's Walt Merton, he's been seeing my roommate Ilyasah," she muttered to Jim. "He's in chemistry." The corners of her mouth turned down. "Look at those kids, they look so serious and awestruck." They began to walk toward the group. "Hi, Walt," Moira said as they approached. "This is Jim Swenson, I don't think you've met." She grinned at the teenagers.

"Hi, Jim," said Walt.

"Jim Swenson the clone?" a small blonde girl asked. Jim looked at her and felt beads of sweat forming on his forehead and under his beard. "Are you the one in astrophysics?"

A wiry dark boy hooted. "How do the profs know which one of you's taking a test?" Jim felt his body tensing. He was immobilized. "My grandmother says you've got mental telepathy," the boy continued, "because you've got one mind." Jim stared at the boy. Dr. Valois had refuted that story long ago, yet people still believed it. He wanted to tell the kids they were being rude. He thought of himself writing a book of etiquette for social relations with clones. "Never reveal to the clone that you do not know who he is." "Tell him how unlike the other clones he is." "Never seat clones on the same side of the dinner table." He restrained the hysterical laugh that almost escaped from his lips.

"I don't have," he managed to say, "telepathy." He turned from the group, aware that both Walt and Moira were looking at him strangely. Then he saw the other man, lurking around an oak tree near the center of the courtyard. He walked away from the group, toward the man. The tiny camera in the man's hand was almost invisible, hidden by his fingers. Jim thought of newsfax pictures, he and Moira in the courtyard, captions: "A Clone in Love," and, in smaller letters, "Can She Tell Them Apart." He stopped in front of the man, grabbed the camera from his hand and smashed it on the tree trunk.

Moira was behind him. "Jim, what are you doing?" She grabbed his arm. The man stared.

"I'll do that," Jim said, "every time I see one of you idiots with a camera!" Moira was tugging at him.

The man sighed. "Young lady, tell this man it is not against the law to study architecture, or photograph buildings." He reached into his pocket and handed Jim a card. "I would appreciate it if you mailed me twenty dollars for the camera, and consider yourself fortunate that I'm not billing you for my wasted time." The man walked away. Jim looked at the card. Herman Steinfeld, Professor of Architecture.

"What's wrong with you?" Moira asked.

He did not answer. He stood there, holding the card, staring past her at the tree.

"I'll see you tomorrow, then," said Moira. Jim hung up the phone and Moira's image disappeared from the small screen.

He wandered into the kitchen and saw Kira sitting at the table, eating a sandwich. The kitchen smelled like a delicatessen. She looked up. He did not want to talk to her. Moira had not stayed on the phone very long, and he had sensed impatience in her voice.

"Want a sandwich?" said Kira, gesturing at the plate of cold cuts in front of her. He could tell that she was worried, and trying to hide it; Kira, when upset, would eat almost compulsively.

"No." He wanted to go to his room. He sat down across the table from Kira.

"Was that Moira? I'd love to talk to her." Kira looked down at the table. "I wish I looked like Moira Buono, too bad Paul's legs weren't a little thinner."

Please shut up, Kira, he thought, and let me sit here in peace, and stop pretending you're worried and trying to cheer me up.

"You should ask her over sometime," said Kira.

Jim shuddered. He thought of Moira meeting his brothers. Ed was studying mathematics, Mike physics and Al astrophysics. Would she be bored by their scientific studies? Would she compare him to them? Perhaps they would all fall in love with her, it was logical to assume that they might. How much real difference was there between them? "It just might be," he said, trying to restrain his anger, "that I want Moira to see me as an individual, not part of an identical herd."

Kira seemed to sense his mood and changed the subject. "I saw Dr. Erman today," she said quickly. "He said you hadn't dialed his poetry discussion in a while, and he wondered . . ."

"Can't you shut up?" said Jim. "You don't have to mind my business for me." His voice was loud, and he looked around, hoping that Al had not heard him.

"I was just . . ." Kira stopped, and continued to watch him. She put down her sandwich. The concern he saw on her face needed no words. She brushed some of the thick brown hair from her forehead.

Jim got up from the table suddenly and hurried out into the living room. Al was seated in one of the booths at the other side of the room, earphones over his head, eyes fixed on the screen. Al was retreating too, into his work rather than from it. Al was a student of astrophysics and was, as a consequence, in competition with the memory of Paul Swenson's work. Paul had laid the theoretical groundwork for a stardrive that would enable humanity to travel beyond the solar system, and Al was suffering doubts, Jim knew, about his ability to do as well. He had applied for a grant to study with the scientists on the moon who were continuing Paul's work, and he did little else but study in the meantime.

Jim turned from the living room and began to climb the staircase to his own room. Al could not be bothered with his worries. He walked to his room and paused at the door. He could hear Ed and Mike talking in Ed's bedroom. They could not be bothered either. Mike was hoping to be able to leave soon for California; he wanted to do advanced work in physics there. Mike wanted to get as far from the other clones as he could, and was determined to make a name for himself apart from the others.

Jim entered his room and closed the door. He flung himself across his bed, trying to hide from the house and the others in it. He lay on the bed, arms hanging uselessly over the side.

He heard the sound of Ed's violin. The music slipped under the door and crept around him, circling mournfully. Ed often relaxed from his studies with music. Paul had done the same, and had enjoyed playing string quartets with Ed and two old friends. One of the old friends had been in the monorail accident that had killed Paul, and now Ed usually played alone.

Jim thought of Ed, Mike, Al and Kira. He saw Kira sitting in the kitchen, pretending concern. She was studying biology and ethics, the only one of the clones actively studying the circumstances that had brought them into being. His mind recoiled at the thought. Keep at it, Kira, he thought, and maybe someday you'll produce something even more monstrous than ourselves.

He lay there, and thought of the pieces of Paul Swenson in the house, fragments of the original man, each emphasizing a different facet of the original. Are we each a whole, he wondered, if one died, would it matter? He rejected the thought, and tried to empty his mind. He was alone.

Jim sat in the chair in Moira's room and stared at the wall. He could not understand what Moira and Ilyasah were saying. Their words were disconnected syllables that he heard but could not interpret.

Moira had seemed annoyed when he showed up at her room that evening. Ilyasah, a student of ancient Egypt, had been sitting in her booth taking part in a discussion. She sat with earphones over her head, encased in the clear plastic cube that was the booth, talking with others who were linked together by the university computer. He had sat in the room quietly while Moira read and Ilyasah spoke to the faces on the screen in front of her.

But Jim had to get out of the house. He had been making notes for a poem when Dr. Aschenbach arrived. Jim had taken one look at the minister's friendly face and decided to leave, quickly. He made his excuses and left the house. Why do you keep coming by, he wanted to ask Jonathan Aschenbach, do you think you can recapture an old friendship with Paul by using us?

Jonathan Aschenbach had been a student of astrophysics with Paul, and had taken several courses in theology, out of curiosity. Paul had told them all how often Jonathan would mock at the religious, but Jonathan had surprised almost everyone by deciding to become a minister. He had helped Paul with some of his research, but most of his time had been taken up with his duties at the Lutheran chapel near the university. Jim knew that Dr. Aschenbach had tried to discourage Paul from taking part in the experiment that had produced the clones. Are you trying to figure out if we have immortal souls, he had wanted to shout at the minister. Instead, he had mumbled something about meeting Moira and had left, driving aimlessly around the campus in his car before deciding to stop at Moira's dormitory.

Jim felt like an intruder. He had nowhere else to go. He couldn't talk to anyone he knew; he felt that others could not really understand him. He couldn't say anything to his brothers or sister. They understood only too well, and had retreated. Jim saw the clones as they must appear to others—identical, a closed group, undifferentiated and inaccessible. Even Kira was almost a mirror image of her four brothers. We're components, interchangeable parts, he thought. He sat and heard the voices of Ilyasah and Moira, background noise that complemented his thoughts. Could Moira, the girl he loved, tell them apart? She had only met Kira. He had never introduced her to his brothers, had never dared. The faces of Ed, Mike, Al and Kira merged in his mind, becoming the same face—that of Paul Swenson.

". . . if they had clones then," said Ilyasah. Jim sat up with a start.

"What," he said, startled, then suddenly realized he had shouted the word. Ilyasah looked surprised, ran her hand over the hair that stood out around her head like a black cloud.

"I was only contemplating," the black girl said. Moira glared at Jim. "I was thinking about what an Egyptian Pharaoh would have done with cloning. Instead of marrying brothers to sisters, they could have insured the purity of the bloodline by . . ." Ilyasah stopped. Jim, almost unaware of his actions, found himself standing over Ilyasah, fists at his sides.

"I was only wondering," Ilyasah said softly. He saw her glance at Moira.

He turned suddenly and left the room, unable to speak. He moved through the curved hallways of the dormitory, suddenly found himself outside next to his car. His hands shook. He looked back at the dormitory and saw Moira standing in the doorway. She had followed him, undoubtedly ready to vent her anger.

Goodbye, Moira, he thought. He had lost her too. He was numb at the thought; it hardly seemed to matter.

He got into the car quickly and drove away from the dormitory, barely noticing the direction he took.

The car hurtled along the automated highway at high speed. The headlights of cars moving on other lanes were bright blurs streaking past him.

Jim huddled in the car, his back against the door, arms around his knees. He was a child again, standing with Mike at the doorway of the bright yellow school building, watching the other children. Some older boys walked toward them; he looked around uncertainly, wondering where Kira, Ed and Al were.

"What's three identical skeletons?" said a large fat boy. "Clone bones," his companions shouted in unison. "What comes in vanilla, vanilla, vanilla and vanilla?" the fat boy went on. "Ice cream clones," said the others. Jim laughed hesitantly, not quite understanding why he was laughing, not quite certain of what the real joke was.

Clone jokes had been popular for a while at the school; most of them had been old ones revived temporarily by some of Jim's classmates, then forgotten again after a month or so.

A buzzer sounded on the dashboard, signaling that his car was approaching the exit he had punched out when he entered the automated highway. The car turned off the highway, moved around the exit bypass, and stopped as it reached a narrow road perpendicular to the exit.

Jim took manual control of the car and turned onto the narrow road. He accelerated recklessly until he could hear the sound of wind rushing past him. He had pushed the vehicle almost to its limit when his buzzer sounded again, signaling danger. The car slowed automatically. He saw the park ahead of him, an isolated wooded area where he and his brothers and sister had gone when they were small. They still went there often, when needing solitude. He drove around the small parking lot in front of the park, and continued into the park along a narrow path. He kept driving, trying to move the car along the path and up a steep hill, until the road became bumpy and he was forced to stop in front of a clump of trees.

Jim got out and walked along the path on foot. The park seemed deserted. Student ecologists had recently finished the restoration of a large wilderness area farther out, and few people continued going to the small park now. Kira had assisted Dr. Takamura in creating cloned eagles for the wilderness. Jim shuddered, thinking of the identical eagles flying over reforested land. He preferred the small park.

He came to a clearing at the top of the hill. A stone wall stood at the edge of the clearing, overlooking the automated highway. He walked toward the wall, stood by it and looked down at the highway two hundred feet below him.

He sat on the wall, dangling his feet over the side. He was a child once more, sitting with the others counting cars on the highway. Mike said they should become a professional basketball team with Paul for a coach. Ed said they would be too short—Paul was not even two meters tall; maybe they better try baseball instead. Kira pointed out that basketball was not yet open to women, most were too short; baseball would be better. Al said they were all strong on pitching, weak on batting, and would have to clone four more people for a team.

Jim thought about his past. They had few other friends as children and had been closer to each other than to anyone else. He thought of Moira and felt pain. He had never grown as close to her as he had once been to the other clones, and knew he never would. She was gone now, he was sure, annoyed by his moods and unable to understand what was torturing him. He saw himself writing a report to Dr. Takamura and Dr. Valois. *The experiment with clones has failed. One of the experimental subjects can no longer live with himself; the others are only four bitter people, denied even the small pleasure of feeling like unique individuals.* He knew they had wanted a team, a Paul Swenson multiplied by five, working together, synthesizing what they learned in different fields, minds so alike they could see connections where others might not.

Jim felt far away from the house where he had grown up, the house that even now was dominated by Paul Swenson's presence. He thought of Paul with bitterness. I'll at least rob you of part of your immortality, he thought, looking down at the highway beneath him. And at last he admitted what he had always known unconsciously: he had been almost relieved at Paul's death, saddened but relieved, freer to go his own way. But he hated himself for the feeling.

It made no difference. He had no real ties to anyone. He would leave only four young people lost in their own worlds, a puzzled psychiatrist who had taken part in an abortive experiment, and a minister trying to recapture an old friendship.

Jim pulled one leg up on the wall, and prepared to leap.

"Jim," called a female voice from behind him. He turned and saw Kira standing near the trees, Dr. Aschenbach at her side.

He groaned. "Kira, leave me alone, please."

She began to walk toward him. He shifted forward on the wall, holding on with one hand. "Get back!" he screamed. "Don't make me jump in front of you, give me that much."

"Wait, Jim," said Kira. She moved forward.

"Stop!" he cried. She halted. "Why are you here? Quite a coincidence, isn't it." He looked from her to Dr. Aschenbach. The stocky minister stood silently behind Kira. "And you," he said to Dr. Aschenbach, "don't you have any other souls to save? You might spend your time better with people you know have them."

Al and Mike appeared behind Dr. Aschenbach. They appeared to have been running. They stopped suddenly. Jim watched the four shadowed figures. Dr. Aschenbach held his hands out, pleading silently. The three clones stood in identical positions, hands clutched to their chests.

Jim found himself chuckling. "What is this, a jamboree?" he shouted. "I'm surprised you didn't bring the newsfax boys, and I don't see Ed around." The four figures were silent. "I guess he has other things to do." His voice was shaking, and he felt tears trickling down his face, losing themselves in his beard. He tried to ignore them. "Well, where is he?" he shrieked. Why should I *care,* he thought.

"He's home," said Kira. "Waiting, in case you went back there." Her face, in the moonlight, seemed shinier than usual; he could see silvery streaks under her eyes.

"For God's sake, will you go!" he cried. Kira began to move toward him. He held up his free hand. Still clinging to the wall, he pulled up both legs, squatted, then stood up, wobbling precariously. He looked back at Kira. She seemed paralyzed. He began to walk along the wall, arms held out for balance.

"Don't do this to yourself," the minister said.

"Save your breath." Jim balanced on one leg. "I wonder why you came to see me die." He stood on two legs again. "Maybe you're just seeing Paul die again, I don't know. Don't worry, old man, you've still got four Pauls left." The tears continued down his face; he didn't seem able to stop them.

He turned from the four people and looked down past his feet at the highway. There were fewer cars on it now. He found himself wondering almost absently whether or not he would land on a car, deciding that his body would land near the edge of the road.

He could hear Kira's voice, although it sounded faint. "Jim, please come down." Mike was saying something too, but Jim could not hear the words.

He poised himself on the wall. Please give me some peace, his mind murmured, let me rest. He thought of the other clones. Forget me, he cried to them silently. *He felt his feet lift off the wall. Silence thundered in his ears. He strained, trying to hear voices, and heard only wind whistling past his ears. He was weightless, arched over a cushion of air, seeing the ground turn under him . . .*

Kira was next to him, one leg over the wall, hand clutching his. She straddled the wall, holding on to him. Her face was streaked with tears. She was shouting something at him, but he could not make out the words. He squatted, then sat on the wall. At last he heard her words.

"Jump, then," said Kira, softly this time. "Jump, but you'll have to take me with you." She continued to cling to his arm. "Go on." He tried to free himself, but she would not let go.

Jim looked down at the highway. The wind was growing cooler and his beard felt cold and wet. Suddenly he found himself shaking with sobs. He clung to Kira. "I've lost Moira," he managed to say, "I know it; clones shouldn't fall in love." He stopped for breath. "And you—you're all strangers."

"No, Jim," said Kira. She released his arm and held his hand gently. "Moira called tonight, she was worried, and she said you were depressed. Why do you think we came here? I knew you'd be here, we always did come when we had to, and poor Ed, he would have come too, except he thought you might come home, and need him." She grasped his hand more tightly. "Can't you see? We need you, Jim, come back with us." Then she was silent.

Jim became aware of the others. Mike and Al had come over to the wall and were leaning against it, watching him. Dr. Aschenbach stood behind them.

"And why are you here?" Jim said to his brothers. "I know what it's like, I look at you every day and see all my gestures, all my features, sometimes even the same thoughts going through your minds. Don't you think I know you feel the same? We're all trying to pretend the others don't exist."

"Maybe we've been wrong, too," said Mike. "I know, sounds funny coming from me. I've been pretty noisy about how I feel." He paused. "Well, I shouldn't have tried so hard. We are different. I'm doing physics. I suppose I have some imagination, but I can't look at a theory and express it in a poem the way you can, or even explain it to people who don't know physics. You can." Mike looked over at Al. "And Al thinks he's competing with Paul, but he isn't really. Paul did his work, now Al'll do his."

"He's right," said Al. "After we study what we have to, there's no reason why we can't work together, the way Paul wanted."

"Certainly," Jim said bitterly. "People expect that of clones. They think we have one mind as it is."

"Oh, Jim," said Kira, "don't you see? People have to work together. If you're apart from them, with no ties, you work only for yourself. People can't live like that. Are any of us so unusual? Don't people all have the same roots anyway? No one's an isolated self, we're all different really, but that doesn't mean we have to isolate ourselves."

Jim was silent. He shivered. The night air had grown very cool. Kira was still watching him. She swung her leg over the wall and stood up. "I'm getting cold," she said. "I guess you have to make your own decision. You know how we feel, but we can't force you." She turned, then looked back. "Please come home, give us a chance, give Moira a chance." She began to walk toward the trees. Al and Mike looked at him uncertainly, then followed her.

Dr. Aschenbach remained. Jim glared at him. "I suppose Paul sat here once and thought of jumping."

The minister shook his head. "No," he said. "I won't say he never got morose, but there were people around who loved him, and he cared about them too. He didn't want to hurt them."

"Didn't he hurt you when he decided to have us cloned?"

"I disagreed with him, but I never doubted that he only wanted to help people. He felt he was under an obligation, call it a Christian one if you will, to use his talents for humanity's benefit. And when he was offered a chance to perpetuate those talents, he took it."

Jim turned from the minister. He looked up at the sky, a starry cathedral curving over the earth. He saw the stars that his father had hoped man would reach one day. "If we stay on earth," Paul had said once, "it's like keeping our eggs in one basket. How little it would take to destroy us all! Shouldn't we try to insure that somewhere in the universe humanity will go on?" Jim began to realize that his father might have had similar reasons for creating five clones, hoping that his concern for humanity would survive in them.

He turned back to the minister, but he had left, disappearing among the trees. There was nothing to prevent him from leaping off the wall now, nothing to stop his escape. It would be quick, a few seconds of soaring over the earth, then oblivion, no chance for thinking or regret. They had left him alone after all. He stood up on the wall and looked down.

No, not alone. They had left him free. They were demonstrating their faith in him, hoping that he would be drawn back to them by love, not coercion.

The scent of pine reached him, wafted to him on the night air. He jumped off the wall and ran toward the trees. "Kira!" he cried. "Al, Mike!" He shouted their names at the trees which stood silently, holding their leafy limbs toward him like welcoming arms. He heard the rustle of underbrush, of running feet.

The four appeared. Kira was the first to run toward him, then Al, then Mike, and Dr. Aschenbach.

He stumbled to them.

mother earth wants you

By PHILIP JOSÉ FARMER

COVEY AND The Man stopped to rest when they got to the top of the high steep hill. Covey looked across the plains below at the little white city several miles away, at the groves of tall trees and the square cornfields and the bright canals and little river. The land was indeed fair.

The Man stood behind Covey, his hand on Covey's shoulder while he spoke softly into his ear. The hand kept squeezing, as if telegraphing a digital code. Whatever the letter of the message, its spirit was nervousness. And no wonder. They were only twenty feet from the sacred grove, where Her power was strongest.

Covey was as nervous as The Man. Wasn't his wife sitting under the central lingam? Wasn't she covered with a blue robe and hood? Wasn't a man approaching her and wouldn't she rise in a moment and drop the robe, revealing a masked face and what the man had to take whether or not he liked what he saw? Once a man crossed the outer ring of trees, he was within sight and sound of Her, and he must go through with the ritual. Otherwise, the earth would tremble and then open up and swallow him. Also gulped down would be the sacred grove and the lingams and Her equipment for seeing and hearing. And Her sacred vessel, Covey's wife. But this did not bother Mother in the least, as far as anybody knew.

The Man, still squeezing Covey's shoulder, said, "Renounce Her! And then you will have the world! The world which She claims to be! But She lies, of course! She does not exist!"

Covey turned around, and the hand fell away. The Man's eyes, irises, pupils, balls, were bright red, as if they had sucked in underground fires and refused to let them go. His hair was shoulder-length, red-bronze, and shimmery in the light of the halo spinning just above the tips of his goat horns. His beard was pale orange; his nose, eaglish. His hands were perforated, and when he lifted one to point upwards, the sky shone through its wide opening.

"There, in the sky, there is where the true deity is."

"Then you know for sure that the priestesses are lying about Her?" Covey said. "She doesn't really exist?"

The Man did not answer. He was fading away into the sunlight. He was Covey's doubts metamorphosed into human shape, though he sometimes seemed more real than Covey himself.

Did The Man really exist? Was he hiding in the woods, begging or stealing bread and wine, sleeping with the foxes in their holes or the sheep in the meadows? Was The Man whom Covey saw the mental projection, the astral forerunner sent by The Man because he was still afraid to expose his flesh and blood where Mother could seize him?

Covey walked towards the grove. The outer ring was composed of twelve times twelve elm trees. The inner ring was seven times nine ash trees. Inside it was a triangle of nine giant oaks. Inside the delta was a round thick shaft of oak painted a reddish pink with blue veinlike lines and topped by a dark red dome creased across the top. Set into each quadrant of the shaft, just below the overhang of the dome, was one of Mother's eyes-ears. The priestesses' technical term for them was "teevee transceivers." Their hidden copper wires went deep, ending in a vein of copper or iron or some similar metal, if Covey had not been misinformed.

From the vein, which was a nerve of Mother Earth, modulated currents flowed. These were shaped by the great brain which could never be seen because it was so deeply buried. It was a brain of stone and metal and was invulnerable, if the priestesses did not lie.

The Man said that they did lie. They were the handmaidens of the Mother of Lies.

But the priestesses said that The Man was the Father of Lies.

The Man said that they had confused him, on purpose, of course, with his own ancient enemy. How clever of Her.

Covey stopped before he quite reached the outer ring. The masked man was rising from Penelope, who lay on the grass with the white legs, the black triangle, the pinkish rings shimmering in the peculiar sunlight that was found only in the sacred groves. The blue mask was still on her face. Anonymity had to be preserved. Mother did not care for personalities. She wanted only the communication of bodies, the most archaic of speech. The only permitted modulations were the curve and angle of protoplasm and the grunts, cries, moans, and the short savage arcs and ellipses and the final vibrations every way free.

The man walked past Covey, removing his mask as he stepped out from under the branches of the outer ring. His expression was both satisfied and religious, as it should have been. He wore a wide-brimmed straw hat, a blue cloak, a bright green kilt, and calf length red boots. He was sweaty and dirty; hay and seeds were stuck in his hair; he stank of horse manure and onions. He looked as if he was a farmer, and he probably was. He had come up from the fields during his lunch hour and, now spiritually refreshed, he was returning to his work. Blessed indeed was he by the Mother.

And the peasant would undoubtedly have good seed. Perhaps he was the one who would provide Penelope with a lusty child.

Penelope had had three children by Covey. Each, living but obviously unhealthy, had been carried by a priestess into the house where, after a short prayer to Mother, she had lifted the infant high so that the eye-ear might see. And, after a few seconds, a single ideogram had appeared on the screen.

The priestess had looked at the white stylized sickle crossed by the five lines representing a sow's head, and she had said loudly what she had read.

"Death!"

And so the baby had been carried to a trough and plunged under water and held there until it was dead. Then it went back into the earth in some field where the roots of wheat or corn would feed upon it.

That was right, and, in the long run, much more merciful. The baby would not grow up to suffer nor would it transmit its imperfections.

It was also right that Covey's wife should sit in the sacred grove and wait for strangers. She had a right to prove that she was not responsible for the sick babies. Or, if she did have a baby by a stranger and it was like the others, then she would have shown that Covey was not at fault. And Covey could then divorce her and get another wife.

He did not want to divorce her, no matter what happened. He loved Penelope with an intensity of which Mother might not have approved if She had known about it. He did not mind too much that his wife sat in the grove. (Or do you? The Man had whispered into his ear more than once.) If she had a healthy child, or if she didn't, she must come back to him.

But Penelope said that she was not coming back. The second day after entering the sacred grove, she had told him that. She would not tell him why. Perhaps, she was ashamed to tell him that she preferred variety. Perhaps, she had become very religious and loved to serve Mother in this way. Perhaps . . . Who knew? All he did know was that she did not want anything more to do with him. Was there something about him that now repulsed her? Did she smell The Man when he appeared? But no, that could not be. The Man had not appeared until after she had told Covey that she wanted no more to do with him.

"Penelope!" he cried.

She sat up and looked around her while the sacred woodpeckers flew up out of the wood in alarm at his shout. She drew her cloak about her, and the sight of the white body withdrawing into the blue cloth made him sick with a frustration of love.

"Penelope! I've come to take you home!"

"What, again?" she said faintly.

He looked up past the blur of her face inside the deep hood at the glassy eye set under the wooden glans of the pillar. His image and his words were being transmitted—who knew how many hundreds or thousands of miles?—to that great brain inside the world. To the brain. No messages could reach Her heart, because She had no heart.

His own heart was a boulder rolling down a steep hill, thudding into other rocks, bouncing, smashing into obstacles, flying off and hitting other rocks, his ribs. His knees were loosened, their pinions removed by his great fear of Mother.

But he shouted at Penelope again. There was no law that a husband could not try to talk his wife out of the sacred grove. As long as he stayed on this side of the outer ring of trees, he was not transgressing.

"Go away!" Penelope said.

"I'll love the child!" he shouted. "You know that! I'll love it just as I love you! And if it turns out that you can't have a healthy child, I still want you! We can adopt a child! Mother only permits each couple to have one child, if it is their flesh and blood! But She permits a couple to adopt as many as they can!"

"I stay here until Mother grants me a healthy child!" Penelope shouted back. "In any event, you and I are through!"

"But why?" he yelled.

She was silent. Perhaps she did not know herself, not that not knowing why she did a thing had ever kept her from giving him a dozen reasons for doing it.

Covey fell silent, and, suddenly, he felt someone behind him. Then a hand was on his shoulder and squeezing dots and dashes. And there was an extra brightness to the sunshine which could only come from the halo.

"Your wife is using the baby as an excuse," The Man whispered. "She likes being a whore. And, since a sacred whore is beyond criticism or censure, she will remain one. Mother Earth protects and feeds her. And so she will stay in the grove until . . ."

"You will become old and ugly!" Covey shouted. "Men will come to you no more! Mother will see what is happening and will kick you out! Where will you go then? I won't be waiting for you! You can work as a house or field hand until you get too old to work and the priestesses of the House of the Sow come for you because you have no one to support you!"

Two men, looking curiously at him from behind their ritual masks, walked by him and under the branches of the outer ring. One was dressed in leather and carried a leather sack full of copper pots and pans on his back. The other wore a cap made of horses' tails and carried a bundle of buggy whips. Such was to be Penelope's lot. Field hands and traveling salesmen, and, on week ends, the unmarried youths and old bachelors from the white city of the plains.

He watched them as they stopped before Penelope, spoke a few words to her, received her blessing, and then sank on their knees for a short prayer to Mother. He continued to watch until they were done. Penelope certainly was pleased with them, and the two seemed to be pleased. One left a large copper pot as a gift and the other gave two buggy whips.

"Why do you watch?" The Man said behind him.

"I can't help it," Covey said. "Penelope is very religious, isn't she? She truly worships Mother with her body."

"Swine!" The Man said, and Covey wondered about this. To call someone a swine was a high compliment. Pigs were sacred to Her, but on special feast days, four times a month, She permitted men to eat them. They were delicious.

The two men left the grove grinning.

"They are laughing at you," The Man said. "They heard you. They know you are her husband."

"Their attitude doesn't seem reverent enough," Covey said.

"No man sneers at another unless he is willing to back up his sneer with his sword," The Man said.

"Mother would see us fight, and She would be displeased, since She did not give us permission."

"Go after them. I bring a sword, not peace, you know," The Man said. "Catch them down the hill, out of Her sight, if you are afraid of Her."

Afterwards, Covey wondered why he had obeyed The Man. He did hate the two, even though he had no right to do so. Yet he could not take out his hatred on them, even if they had not seemed reverent and should have been chastised.

Later, he would see the contradiction. Why get angry at men who lacked reverence when he was so doubtful about Mother himself?

But he wasn't being logical, and he did need a vent for his anger. He followed the two down the path, calling after them when all three were out of Mother's sight. They turned, and, seeing his angry face, started to draw their swords. Doubtless, they had intended only to warn him off. At that moment, however, he needed the slightest excuse to attack, and he thought he had it.

"Draw on me, will you?" he shouted. "Wasn't having my wife enough?"

The latter must have startled them, since it sounded so irrational to them. They were slow in their responses, perhaps because the fear of madness made them cautious. They may have thought it would be better to try to talk him out of his madness.

Covey slashed at them, cutting one's neck in half and chopping off the sword hand of the other.

Afterwards, he grew sick. He did not vomit because of their blue faces or the blood. Mother's children saw much of the butchery of animals and of voluntary human sacrifices. The cat clawing inside his belly was the thought that these two had just left a religious service and he had allowed his secular feelings to interfere with Her worship.

Or had he, he asked himself as he began to recover from his sickness? The service had been completed; the men had left the holy ground.

But all ground was holy, since all earth formed Mother's breasts.

Some ground was more holy than others, however.

The Man, looking down on the bodies, said, "This is the first step in the war against Her."

"I wish you wouldn't say things like that," Covey whispered. "They scare me."

He was more than scared. He wanted to run and run until he was out of sight of the hill and the dead men. But he would never be out of sight of Mother. No matter how carefully he moved around, sooner or later he would come within view of one of Her eyes.

How had he gotten into this horror?

"Horror is the daughter of doubt," The Man said.

"I notice you said *daughter*, not *son*," Covey replied.

"It's important to make such distinctions," The Man said. "Distinctions are the guideposts along the road to truth."

The Man seemed to be getting more solid. The sunlight was running into obstacles inside his image. It was bouncing back and back as if it glanced off crystals forming in his body. Perhaps The Man was a ghost and fed off the blood of living things.

Perhaps, though, The Man was what he claimed to be. Perhaps he wasn't just the exteriorized persona of the man-god which sleeps in the lower brain of every human being. Mother had striven to put this Man to sleep forever. But he would not lie down and sleep; he must be up and out.

Covey wished again that he had not been chosen as the vehicle for the return of The Man. How easy to believe wholeheartedly in Mother, to sink down on your knees before Her sacred trees and Her eyes-ears and cry out to Her and then see Her answers to your prayers on the screens, the flickering ideograms which said Yes or No and, almost always, Go with my blessing, my son.

Mother had so much more to give than The Man. She was the whole earth, and she fed and clothed Covey and gave him stone and wood for house and fire and the beasts of the field to ride and to eat and to work for him and gave him Her daughter to be his wife. (However, as The Man pointed out, She also took all this away if She felt like it.) Whereas, The Man was the son of the beaten and discredited god of the sky. True, without air, life was not. But even this precious element came from Mother. Without Her grass and trees, air would become poison. So, even The Man and his father had lived only at Mother's sufferance. They had ruled at Her sufferance, too, though you would never have known it if you believed their arrogant boasts.

Long long long ago, so the priestesses said, Mother had ruled over all Her body. And then evil arose, and the men of the North and the desert tribes turned to their own image and formed from worship of themselves the father god and, eventually, his son. They slew the worshippers of Mother in their own lands and then they swarmed out of their lands into other lands. And, eventually, they killed or forcibly converted the worshippers of Mother. But a few of Her people survived, living in the midst of the father-god worshippers and disguised as such.

Mother was patient. She waited. And man invented science and he flourished and multiplied. Beyond reason. And then Mother Herself: Her waters, Her soil, Her air, became poisoned.

About this time, so the priestesses said, women began to throw off the patriarchal yoke. And a woman discovered that Earth was not just a ball of matter circling the sun. She was a sentient being, a self-conscious entity. She had blood and bone, organs, a skin, and a brain. Or the mineral analogs of such.

Mother Earth, it was discovered, talked. The puzzling configurations of electromagnetic fields which supersensitive instruments had detected were words of Her language. She was transceiving to-from the moon and the other planets. Mother Earth and hot little Mercury and hot mist-hidden Venus and little red Mars and the vast icy remote giants Jupiter, Saturn, and Uranus, and the even icier and more remote Neptune and Pluto, talked.

And so the scientists decoded the speech of the spheres (no easy task because of the scarcity of recognizable referents), and they assigned ideograms to the units of the language.

The next step was to talk to Mother Earth Herself.

Meanwhile (as the priestesses said), mankind was dying. Man was killing himself off in his own poisons, dying in his self-fouled nest.

Mother Earth twitched Her skin.

In other words, She generated earthquakes, sank lands, and lifted oceans.

The survivors swore they would never again offend Mother.

The only science permitted now, or, to be more exact, technology, was that needed to make and maintain the electronic equipment to communicate with Mother. Hence, the sacred groves and temples, the phallic pillars and the glassy eyes-ears of Mother. Hence, the abhorrence of all but the simplest machinery needed to plow Mother's skin. Hence, the rule of state and church by women. Hence, the passing of tolerance, for it was only when faith weakened that tolerance for other faiths was born. But if a faith have the truth, then it should not put up with anything that denies the truth.

All this had seemed to Covey, at one time, to be the way things should be. And Covey was still not sure that it wasn't the way things should be.

But, one day, he had walked by the great grave-shaped hill where the body of the father god was said to lie. Never mind that other areas had similar graves with similar claims. Covey had looked once at the hill and then turned his gaze away. The gigantic body interred in there had long ago rotted. But the bones must still nourish evil, and it was best not to loiter in their neighborhood. And then, as he strode along the base of the hill, anxious to get away, his eyes averted, he saw The Man rise from the earth and stand before him.

Terror had locked the joints of his skeleton. Here was the ancient enemy who would not stay down. Or, at least, the son of the enemy. Covey was confused about which was father and which was son, since the priestesses who taught school did not seem to know the distinction themselves. At least, if they did, they had never made it clear.

Since that day, Covey had not been able to get rid of The Man.

Perhaps it was The Man who was responsible for the troubles between Penelope and Covey. The Man denied this. He said that it was Mother who had caused them. She was the one who insisted that a woman should have the last word in everything. Whereas, the man should be the head of the family, the state, the church. Women should be subservient to their natural lords. As for the thing called equality, forget that. Equality existed only in mathematics. Wherever two or more were, there was also a pecking order.

Naturally, so The Man said, Mother favored women. She felt closer to beings of Her own sex. Yes, Mother Earth, even if She were a planet, a massy ball of rocks and iron and soil and water and air, was a female.

But who, then, was the father? Who seeded Her, who planted in Her womb?

Covey did not argue about that. Mother was a woman. No doubt of that. As a child, and even more as a juvenile, he had had his dreams of Mother coming to him through the blackness of the night. She was a tall woman, mountainously breasted, massively buttocked, hugely thighed. She was blonde, and She was white everywhere except for the dark cavernous delta. Even Her eyes were pale.

The schoolchildren were encouraged to describe their nocturnal encounters, and the juveniles told in class of their couplings with Mother, their ecstatic emissions.

Sometimes, the boys saw Her as the queen of the land. The queen was a woman they had seen in the flesh when they went to the great white city to the east, and so she was easily visualized. But it was understood that she was not the queen when she appeared in dreams. She was the symbol of Mother, of course.

The girls dreamed of lying with the king, who sat on a throne lower than the queen's and who was sacrificed when his manly vigor ran out. But the girls understood that he was a symbol of Mother, though a third-hand one, in a sense. Sometimes, the girls told of meeting Mother in their dreams and of being embraced, held against those brobdingnagian breasts, and of sucking. The wonderful milk refreshed them, and they went back to dreaming of the king.

And what of Covey's dreams of The Man?

They had all been nightmares.

The Man had explained that this came about because of the conflict in Covey's mind. Once he had rid himself of his evil love for Mother, then the nightmares would go away.

"When my father ruled, Mother used to come to man in his dreams as a terrible hag or a lovely vampire," The Man said. "Now that She is ascendant, She sees to it that my father, and myself, play the role that my father once gave to Her."

Definitions meant nothing now. Only deeds mattered. And the deed was done. He had murdered two men.

"You have three choices," The Man said. "You can run and hide and try to form an underground. You can run and take refuge in the fairy reservation. Or you can throw yourself on Mother's mercy.

"Let's take the last two first. The reservation is for homosexuals and criminals who want a sanctuary. But it's not much of a refuge, since, every now and then, Her soldiers come in and thin down the population, just as the forest rangers crop the deer population when it's too large.

"You can throw yourself on Her mercy. The lightest sentence you could get would be to serve as a eunuch priest in one of Her temples. There you can swing censers and sweep floors and develop all of the vices and none of the virtues of a woman.

"You can become an outlaw, and you can find others who dream of The Man, and, in time, you can start a revolt against Mother. Believe me, there are many men like you. With enough of them, you could destroy the sacred groves, rip out Her eyes-ears, make Her deaf, dumb, and blind, and render Her helpless. And then you will see how easy it is to overcome women when you have the muscle and they lack Mother's direct help."

While Covey stood in thought, he had control of events taken from his hands—if he had ever had any control. A woman screamed. Below him was a woman clad in a blue robe and hood. She must have come up to sit also in the sacred grove, but she had almost stepped on the two bodies. Now, after screaming three times, she turned and ran back down the path.

Covey overtook her, and, knowing that words were useless, cut her head off.

The Man, standing behind him, said, "The blood of my father's enemies feeds him. I hear him stirring in his grave."

"And what will my blood, when it is spilled, do for him?" Covey said.

"The blood of his martyrs is like a sea that's broken a dike. It spreads his worship."

Covey felt as if he were a chess piece. First, Mother moved him. Then, The Man. Then, Mother. And so on.

"And my father can do more for you than Mother," The Man said. "She promises only that you will be born, will live a while, may have a happy life if you follow Her laws, and then will assuredly die forever. I can promise you a life after death."

"Can you keep that promise?" Covey said.

The Man was silent, and, when Covey turned, he saw that he was fading away again.

Covey sliced off the men's genitalia, climbed back up the hill, entered the grove, and cast down his offerings at the feet of Penelope, though they were to Mother, not to her.

"Mercy, Mother!" he said. "I have killed two of your sons and one of your daughters! I was mad! Because of love of a woman!"

She would surely understand that.

"And I have come to my Mother because She promises only what She can fulfill! Out of Her womb we come, and back into Her womb we go! And that is all She offers, because that is all there is!"

Penelope had moved away until her back was against the lingam. She stared at the bloody organs and the bloody sword. Surely, Covey thought, she must know that if Mother says I am to die, then she will die, too.

Covey waited. And he felt a faint stirring behind him, something light and airy but still solid enough to displace some air. Had The Man dared to materialize within the sacred grove?

If Mother saw The Man standing behind him, She would have no mercy at all.

He turned. The sunlight was being troubled by an alien presence. Mists were forming. The beams were being refracted and reflected.

"Go away!" Covey said. "Are you mad?"

"Do not be afraid," a thin voice said. "I am with you."

"That is what makes me afraid," Covey said, but he faced the lingam again. At that moment, as if She had been waiting for him to see, She flashed the ideogram for death upon Her eye. It flickered in and out. "Death! Death! Death!"

A hand clamped down on his shoulder. The Man said, "Do not die like an ox or a lamb! Battle like a hero! And, who knows, you may get away and collect others like you around you! There are plenty who dream of The Man and of his father stirring in his grave."

Covey shouted and swung his blade. Penelope's scream was cut off, as was her head. Covey picked up a large rock and heaved it. It shattered Mother's eye-ear so that She would not be able to see him running off down the hill. Not that that mattered, since the other eyes would know that he could have gone in only one direction, inasmuch as they had not seen him.

Covey ran down the hill and along the dirt road and then across fields and meadows and through woods and across brooks and ravines. At each second he expected the earth to shake and to crack around him and perhaps under him. He had hoped that She would be in a rage and shatter the earth for miles around Her. To kill one, She would kill a thousand innocents. Too bad. So much the worse for them. But they could be replaced, and the survivors would fear Mother's anger even more.

Covey was hoping that She would lose Her temper. He would take his chances on being wiped out in the general catastrophe. And if he escaped, he would then have put a number of Her eyes-ears out of commission. While the techs were repairing the damage, he would be at the next sacred grove, upsetting Her and causing Her to strip Herself of Her own communications.

The Man, running along behind him, said, "Wait a minute! Use your brains! Think! You can't do much by yourself. But if you got a large enough gang, and they made Mother destroy Her own eyes-ears over a large enough area, then She would be rendered deaf, dumb, and blind. And you'd have a chance to do something against the army She'd send in. You might even eventually strip Her of all Her senses. Then She would be helpless. She would rage and cause widespread destruction, perhaps, but after a while She'd forget. And mankind could walk unafraid over Her breast. And men would regain their natural place in society."

"I'll think about it," Covey said. "But why hasn't She quaked this area? What is She thinking of?"

The Man told him to stay away from the sacred groves until he had gotten enough converts to test Her strength. Covey waved him away. His curiosity was too strong. He had to find out what She was up to. Who knew but what She had decided to ignore human beings all of a sudden? Perhaps She had tired of this tiny breed of monsters that was always pestering Her.

"You're crazy!" The Man said. "I know the old Bitch from a long way back. Mark my words. . . ."

Towards evening, Covey found another hill on top of which was a sacred grove. He climbed it with his plan and determination hardened. He would kill the sacred whore, or whores, he found under the pillar. He would allow Mother to see him do it, and then he would run. Surely, this time, She would break open the earth for miles around. But he would escape; he was convinced of that.

"You're suffering from guilt and you want to die!" The Man said.

fallen on the land below and darkened somewhat the grove. At the foot of the lingam sat a shrouded figure.

Covey did not put on his cloak or mask. He would let Mother know he was coming, let Her have time to get angry.

The figure stood up as he neared it. It dropped the cloak.

Her body was white and beautiful.

She dropped her mask, and he saw a skull.

He yelled with horror and then cried, "Mother Death!"

His momentary inaction had given her the chance to use the weapon, or ritual tool, that she had hidden behind her. The sickle cut through his members with a single stroke.

Other figures emerged from the gloom of the trees beyond. They seized him and carried him off while the priestess removed the skull mask. She was beautiful; she had long honey-colored hair, lips as red as blood, and wild staring eyes.

She stooped and picked up his genitals, held them up so that Mother could see them, and tossed them upon his belly.

The man holding his legs got between him and the woman, and Covey saw her no more. But there was little more he would ever see. The shock and the loss of blood were carrying him off even faster than the eunuch priests.

"A corner of a field down there needs feeding," one of his carriers said.

The other grunted.

Covey felt a hand on his shoulder. He saw, as if it were smoke passing, The Man.

"She's a wily old Bitch," The Man said. "She's learned that She just hurts Herself if She rips up the earth to get at one person. So She sent a daughter after you. Or sent one to wait for you, rather."

The darkness was almost complete. He seemed to be riding as a passenger, a very small passenger, in his own head.

"You will die, too," he said to The Man. "You were born of me. I couldn't have children, so I conceived you. You will die when I die."

The panic in The Man's voice was only the ghost of panic. But Covey felt it strongly.

No! I exist! I am an idea! Ideas aren't born in a mind! They float around, and they enter a mind if there is an opening for them.

Covey was too small and weak to reply. Mother had been weeding out men like himself, slowly, generation after generation, but surely.

And he was the last of his kind. With him would die The Man. The idea even of The Man.

Both of them, however, would be of some use. The corn would appreciate them; the earth would be richer for a long time to come because of them.

Mother knew best.

chronicles of a comer

By K. M. O'DONNELL

SEPTEMBER 14: Harder and harder to concentrate upon the demographic urges of Dayton, Ohio, that most American of the American cities. Fourteen percent of college-educated housewives believe in stronger repressive measures against the drug-culture; fifty-one percent of working-class males above the median in salary believe that television is a government plot. Etc. Sitting here, the figures heaped before me, graphing them out slowly and neatly into the presentation brochures I feel a sense of uselessness overcoming me unlike any I have ever known . . . and I have often felt useless. What does it matter? Who cares? What would the working class of males say to my condition? I believe in the Second Coming.

I believe in the Second Coming. Putting down this sentence in the journal of my thoughts and activities I have just decided to keep, I feel a thrill of sheer madness going through me; a throbbing unleashed that causes me to literally shift in place, cover this entry apprehensively lest a strolling Supervisor wander through to peer down at my work and see what has been written. *I believe in the Second Coming.* Perhaps I should seek psychiatric help which is at least partially covered by the company benefit program. Nevertheless I do. Indications point to it. Breakdown, dislocation, strange noises and rising from the East; assassination, great alienation and discontent, the scar of barbarism opening up deep within the layers of the culture. Conditions force. According to the most informed readings of the Book of Daniel it will occur within the next ten years; then again, according to other discredited authorities, it might have happened in 1928. No matter, no matter. It will happen. A small pulse of necessity flowers within me, guiding my hand through this entry and as if from a far distance I hear the bell of Apocalypse striking.

I wonder what form He will take so that, as promised, all witnessing will know Him.

September 15: Failure with Francine again tonight. Our marriage has arced downward, a clear bell curve of declension in recent months, now I can no longer bear to touch her. Preoccupied with the larger considerations of last judgment I cannot concentrate upon her any more; cannot even take our troubles seriously. "You don't care," she says, "you don't care about people. You're just a cold-hearted statistician who sees people as numbers and trends. You fooled me for a while but that's all you ever were. You do not care."

She is right but she is wrong. I do not care about people (because they will merely bear witness to the Coming) but I am not a cold-hearted statistician. More and more, the devices of my work seem insane to me: what does Kettering or Dayton, Ohio have to do with the high, pure cleaning flame, the clean arching notes of the trumpet signalling time come around again? It is hard to believe that I ever took this seriously. That I ever took Francine seriously. Tonight I tried, however.

I took her to dinner, listened to her little complaints and held my peace for the evening, brought her back to the apartment finally and, willing myself to focus, touched her, pressed my palms against her, removed her clothing and mounted her like a crucifix. How long, how long it had truly been since I felt desire! But even as we rocked together I felt that desire perishing; my mind scurrying off into a small abscess where I saw and heard the form that last judgment would take and where our pitiful little struggles would stand, against the bar of Heaven.

I slid off her in revulsion, closing my eyes and denying the seed. Behind me she said things which I would not hear. I have failed with her before but never for reasons so justified and now I am in a high, cold place where she cannot touch me. I do not care whether she leaves or not.

September 16: At lunch hour today, a quick walk on Lexington Avenue to restore the circulation, brush thoughts of Dayton machinists and schoolchildren from my mind. In the doorways prostitutes, beggars, the obscurely displaced of the city whom I once fantasized kept the machinery going through the principles of necessary inefficiency. "Give me some money, you," a particularly vicious beggar said to me as I stepped out across Twenty-fourth Street, "who do you think you are?"

The impulse for flight quickly cancelled, I turned upon the beggar ready for confrontation . . . and then it occurred to me in a great burst of light that there was no saying what form He will take upon His ascension; He is as likely to be a beggar as to return in more glorious forms. Quickly, I searched the creature's face for indications of sacrament but could detect nothing but loathing and aggression. Still, how are we to know? Can we judge at this plane the devices of the saints? "Are you . . ." I started to say and then balked to an embarrassed muteness. I realized that I was about to ask the beggar if he were the Saviour.

"My God," he said, "I think you're crazy," and sprinted from me quickly, turning a corner and being gone. In the distance I heard an explosion which might have been the backfire of a bus or the sound of the beggar reassuming his natural form and going to a High Place. Who can tell? What is there to know? I continued meditating on my way, unable to escape the exciting feeling which has come over me since I started this journal. I am in the midst of climactic events.

September 17: Nothing happened today. Air thick, oppressive, damping down upon the city; news of the shooting of yet another Presidential candidate. Indications accelerate. Francine left me today. She was not at the apartment when I returned. She had removed her clothing and I discarded her note without reading.

September 18: Problems at the company. Called into the supervisor's office this morning; told that my work had been falling off seriously in recent weeks. Simple statistical errors, flaws of computation a child would not have made, misplacement of median and mode. "We cannot tolerate this kind of thing," the supervisor went on to say (am omitting proper names from this journal as much as possible; Francine's only mentioned because she has no effect upon my life), "precision, grace, close tolerances, market research, dependent advertisers, key demographics," and so on and with a final admonition sent me from his office with the clear indication that career and salary plan or not, my position may be considered somewhat endangered at the present time.

What would it benefit him if I told the basis for my distraction, outlined my conviction that very little can be taken seriously at the present moment since time itself is ending? He would not understand and my job would be further endangered and then again, more terrifyingly, he might understand perfectly and his bland, blank eyes would focus upon me in perfect stillness and peace, all of his features rotating toward waxy flexibility. "Just tell me how soon," he would say then in a little voice, "that's all I want to know. How soon because really, I too cannot take this any more."

September 19: At lunch hour I think I saw the beggar again but then I am not sure; he fled so quickly when our paths intersected on the sidewalk. "What's wrong with you?" a voice said to me while I was walking abstractedly, "anyway, give me all your money," but as I turned to the sound he must have recognized me and whisked away. Maybe. Perhaps. It does not explain the source of his terror (unless any knowledge of his true identity would shift the Plans) nor does it bring me any closer to a pinpointing of the date when he may be expected to shed his earthly mask and appear before us in His true substance.

Utterly missed a distribution curve today and had to redo an entire chart. I agree. My work is not what it once was.

September 20: The wounded Presidential candidate may recover. Then again he may not. It is difficult to make a medical judgment at this time; fortunately he is a minor party candidate so the true course of the election has not been affected. Candidates from the major parties have reduced their speaking schedules to closed auditoriums and security has been tightened even further. Two Eastern nations, through the proxies of their Heads of State, have declared a final war. The President, himself not a candidate for re-election, has appeared on television urging calm. In Dayton the appeal has been met with apparent calm. The indications quicken; the world is a great artery being brought to the knife.

Francine reappeared. "I thought you would worry," she said, "I thought you would try to find me. I thought you would read my note and understand that I only left you out of desperation and wanted to shock you into understanding. But now I realize that I was wrong all the time and that there is nothing there. This is the last time. I am coming only to pick up my last things; my lawyer will hear of this and he will be in touch with you. Do not speak to me. You didn't even read my note, did you?"

There is nothing to say to her. I have nothing to say to her. While she bangs around the apartment, muttering, I sit in a corner of the living room, in a chair, and read the newspapers carrying further reports of the wondrous signs and portents. It occurs to me that perhaps I should check her out more carefully, at least to see if there is any possibility that He is made manifest in her . . . but that is clearly impossible. This at least I know if I know nothing else; He would not return to earth in the form of a woman.

September 21: Forty-three percent of central America disapproves of the shooting of even minor candidates for President, tentative conclusion. Disapproval is highest among college graduates, lower as expected in those with only a high school education. There is a coefficient of correlation of .85 between approval of the shooting of bizarre candidates and a belief in the immorality of pre-marital sexual intercourse. I do not know what to make of this nor are my speculations needed. I convey the figures, the charts, the random patterning, the tentative graphs to my supervisor who looks at them quizzically and says that they will have to be forwarded on for further processing.

At lunch hour I look for the beggar who has become an important part of my life but do not see him. Perhaps He is already at this moment in seclusion, preparing His garments for the Ascension and no longer walking to and fro in the Earth or upon it as He prepares for His enormous tasks.

September 22: He will come wearing a crown of fire, He will come from the high place and stand above us, He will bring down His hand

and signal the beginning of the one thousand years of destruction which must precede His eternal reign but even knowing this, I am calm; time has come around again, we can no longer tolerate what has become of us. My belief has become my armor; in its coolness I dwell, acceptance of the spirit, no trembling of the flesh and when He brings down His hand then to start the fires I will stand among the steadfast, calm in the righteousness of my vision, protected by the depth of my acceptance.

One of the wounded candidates passed into a coma this morning and is not expected to recover. Bombs are falling upon the nations of the East and no quick conclusion to the war is expected. In the mails this morning arrived a letter from a man representing himself to be Francine's lawyer, asking for a full accounting of my position. I wish, I only wish that I could share it with him.

September 23: Dayton, Ohio reacts, according to the first quick surveys, with great calm to the death of the unfortunate Presidential candidate. The coefficient of correlation between acceptance of his death and the belief in a really effective headache remedy appears to be upwards of .75. These conclusions will be telephoned immediately to our client, the headache remedy company. "It's a crazy business," my superior says (he has moments of recrimination), shaking his head, and I do not have the heart to tell him that soon his business, along with everything else, will be no more. Like so many of us, like the way I used to, he holds onto the devices of his life as if they were imperishable artifacts bridging or containing all reality; I would not take this away from him. In time he too will accept the judgment. For now he contents himself with verifying and transmitting the tentative conclusions as locked to my desk I work my pencil through the forms and look out the window occasionally, waiting for the first glimpse of that rosy haze which, I know, will signal culmination.

September 24:

September 25:

September 26: Still too weak to write today. Maybe tomorrow. Oh my God.

September 27: I did nothing; he fell upon me like a beast and oh my Lord my body is a wound. Tomorrow. Tomorrow I will be better. I will write more tomorrow. At least I did not have to be hospitalized although the company would have covered everything.

September 28: Stronger, but inside broken. The end of the weekend which coincided with the attack so at least I did not miss more than three days of work. Back in the office tomorrow. Everyone very sympathetic. Even Francine called, but when she found that the injuries were essentially superficial and limited to what is laughingly called "cuts and abrasions" she hung up.

September 29: I do not know how I feel about the beggar, now that he has beaten me. Today, driven by an impulse I could not understand, I visited him in the security ward where he is being held for observation. He made no attempt to escape after the beating, merely standing over me and muttering strange threats while the large crowd which had gathered parted for the police to take him easily. "Why?" I asked him through the little window, "why did you do it? I would have given you money. I would have . . ." In my mouth are the words: *I would have given you anything if you had asked; I thought you were the Saviour,* but I do not say them. After all, I am in a mental hospital; our conversation monitored. Also, I am not sure that I believe this any more. Everything that has happened to me in the last months, everything that I was thinking, seems to have been a strange illness that was battered from me; not only my blood but convictions poured on the stones. "Why?" I said again weakly.

The beggar said nothing. His eyes cold and empty, his hands rigid on the panels, his body a withdrawal. Nothing, nothing. Is it possible that he was a simple lunatic from the beginning, the beating merely because I became a focus by our constant interception of paths? Or has something gone away from him; that which I suspected never to be touched?

It does not matter. I left, telling the authorities on the way out that no, I would not press charges if the beggar were confined for a long, long time.

No rising, no fire, no music, no thousand years of destruction. Only this grey inelegance but looking through the trap of choices, I see that it could have been no other way. We are not for the quick-fire.

September 30: The President was shot in the shoulder while leaving a press-conference. The assailant has been seized; a foreigner from the East protesting the President's policy of non-involvement in the war. He seems barely coherent but is perhaps merely excited. The shot narrowly missed the President's temple at close range but due to the fortunate escape, he is expected to be back at his desk within the week. Already he is conducting business from his hospital bed and has released a statement to the nation calling for calm.

Another call from Francine tonight, sounding much calmer herself, as if the near-assassination had deeply touched her. She said she felt guilty in some way for my severe beating and wondered if somehow, some way, we could make another try at our marriage.

I told her that we would see. Tonight, she is supposed to spend the evening with me. The thoughts are less tormenting than they have been for months and I think that I may, if circumstances turn a certain way, be able to function. I want to function; it is the least that I could do in line with the gravity of events and with the President's appeal.

October 14: Only a few weeks but September seems so far from me now. A different world; an enclosure from which I have been sprung. Francine has come back to live with me; my work is becoming meaningful again, the word from the networks and newspapers merely uncomfortable but no longer signs and portents. The beggar has been found insane and remanded upstate. It does not seem to have happened. Reality has once again overtaken me; joyfully I will confront it.

This morning, at the agency, working on skewed responses in Dayton to the President's quick and astonishing recovery, I thought once again that I saw a vision of the Coming but it was not as it had been before and not as it had ever been in my life. Looking at the charts, the figures, the slow curves being traced out, I thought I saw in that lovely coldness, entrapped in peace forever, the face of the Saviour, and the joy that I felt as I moved the pencil to capture the details, the vaulting of the heart as I saw him pure before me in the forty-seven percent of Dayton that no longer accepts the teachings of any Church . . . this arc of happiness took me like grace and falling all the way down, I sung the sound of Gabriel.

Roger Elwood has been a science fiction editor for eight years and in that length of time has compiled a credit list of nearly 60 books. These have ranged from juvenile anthologies to the most sophisticated and controversial adult books [A recent one includes serious explorations of such themes as homosexuality, gorgonism, pollution, mass hypnosis, white-black relationships and so on.]. One recent anthology entitled *The Young Demons* was termed "a treasure" by noted author-reviewer Theodore Sturgeon who added that it was the best anthology of its type since William Tenn's *Children of Wonder,* the latter considered a hallmark work. Elwood recently concluded an agreement to edit with Robert Silverberg the biggest science fiction anthology ever created; it will total some 280,000–300,000 words. Elwood resides in Margate, New Jersey—and is at work on books for a number of other publishers.